AN AUTU

AN AUTUMN LIFE

*How a surgeon faced
his fatal illness*

Ethel Helman

faber and faber

LONDON · BOSTON

First published in 1986
by Faber and Faber Limited
3 Queen Square London WC1N 3AU

Filmset by Goodfellow & Egan, Cambridge
Printed in Great Britain by
Redwood Burn Ltd Trowbridge Wiltshire
All rights reserved

British Library Cataloguing in Publication Data

Helman, Ethel
An autumn life: how a surgeon faced his fatal illness.
1. Cancer—Patients—Biography   2. Terminally ill—Biography
I. Title
155.937   362.1′96994′00924   RC263
ISBN 0-571-13704-0

Library of Congress Cataloging in Publication Data

Helman, Ethel.
An autumn life.
1. Helman, Percy—Health.   2. Surgeons—South Africa—Biography.
3.   Cancer—Patients—South Africa—Biography.
I. Title
RD27.35.H45H45   1986   362.1′96994 [B]   85-20752
ISBN 0-571-13704-0 (pbk.)

Contents

Acknowledgements

This book would not have been written without the encouragement of my children, who together with David and Dudley made such a valuable contribution. It has reached publication under the guidance and skill of Patricia Downie and Elizabeth Bland. Throughout the whole period of writing and being published I have been supported by many friends. To all these people I now extend my grateful thanks.

The obituary, quoted on page 94, is reproduced from *Clinical Oncology*, 1982, 8, 383–4, by permission of the publishers, Academic Press Inc. (London) Ltd, and the writer, Mr R.W. Raven OBE, TD, FRCS, to whom the author and publishers extend their thanks.

Introduction

Many people say, at some time in their lives, 'If only I could write . . .' I never had any such aspirations. The prospect of writing a book would not have crossed my mind had fate not taken a particular turn at a time in our lives when my husband and I thought we could at last relax and enjoy the fruits of all our earlier endeavours.

My husband, Percy, was a surgeon who spent the major part of his life treating patients with cancer. Some were cured; some were palliated; some died. To all he willingly offered his surgical skill. More especially, he cared about all of them.

At the height of his career he diagnosed his own cancer, and over the course of the next twenty months he recorded his reactions on tapes. After his death I found the tapes, and it is my honest belief that he wished me to use them in some way to help others. Although he was always a compassionate man, I think he became aware, through his illness, of feelings that he had not considered before. I believe he hoped that his own experiences might help other patients to cope with their bewilderment, pain and fear and to overcome the sense of isolation that severe illness often brings with it. I think he also hoped that doctors and other medical professionals, as well as family and friends, could learn from his observations.

The idea for this book developed while I was keeping my eleven-year-old grandson, Adie, company when he was in bed with a fever. I had never had a real discussion with him before and was surprised by the thoughts in his mind.

'What are you typing, Granny?' he asked.

'I'm typing the story of Grandpa's illness, darling.'

'Is that called a biography?'

'I suppose so, in a way.'

'But how can you write a biography about Grandpa? He wasn't a very famous man, was he?'

'No, my darling, he wasn't very famous, but he was very special. I want you to realize that everyone is special to someone.'

'He was a doctor, Granny. Why did he get cancer?'

'We have no control over the diseases we get, darling, and Grandpa knew that very well. He spent most of his life helping people with cancer, and when he became ill he made some tapes describing how he felt. I think he hoped that they would help other people who were suffering.'

'Do all people who get cancer die, Granny?'

'No, my darling, cancer is not one disease but many, just like any other illness. Some people do die, but lots of others remain well for a long, long time, and many people are completely cured.'

That seemed to satisfy Adie, and he went on reading his comics.

Percy's tapes form the focal point of the story, which, though sad, is full of courage, hope and dignity. For a man who had acquired an international reputation as a surgeon, and who was involved in worldwide research into cancer treatments, it was an irony of fate that he should be afflicted with the disease himself. Although the tapes are to some extent a medical record, as might be expected in Percy's case, they reveal too his love for his family and his desire to live his life as fully as possible, and they indicate that he anguished over the issues that concern everyone: who would do his work during his illness? Would his job be kept for him? Would we, his family, be able to manage?

If there is one lesson above all others to be learned from Percy's tapes, it is that we should allow those who are close to us to share our fears, our loneliness and our hopes. We should also be ready to talk openly to family, friends and medical advisers, so that we can build relationships based on honesty and trust.

The Groote Schuur Hospital was held in great esteem and affection by Percy. In return, he was regarded as a much loved father figure by his colleagues, whom he considered his greatest friends. Their care for Percy, and their concern for my family and for me during his illness and after his death, are kindnesses for which I can never adequately thank them.   E. H., 1986

Early Years 1924–47

Percy was an ordinary man in the sense that he was similar to many others with normal hopes and aspirations. He was born on 1 January 1924 in the small village of Laingsburg, which is in the Karoo in the Cape. He was proud of being a Karoo *seun* (son). Laingsburg is approximately 300 kilometres from Cape Town, which today seems near but then, without tarred roads and with difficult mountain passes, seemed very isolated.

The first sixteen years of his life were very different from those of a young boy growing up in a big city. I have always been attracted to people from the country, as they seem to have an added dimension to their personalities. Although they are deprived of urban entertainments and certain aspects of culture, they develop a depth of character and personal involvement with each other which is devoid of guile or malice. They really share their lives with the people with whom they come into contact, and this close relationship with family and friends remains an integral part of their lives. This shared community life gives a certain security to young people brought up in the country, which enables them to have an astute sense of values in later life.

Percy's grandfather emigrated from a small town in Lithuania because conditions had become intolerable for the Jews under the rule of the Tsar. Like so many other immigrant Jews without means and with very few possessions and unable to speak either of the two official languages, English and Afrikaans, he arrived in South Africa hoping to make a living. Regardless of their previous culture or experience, the immigrants had to find work. Consequently, many of them were forced to become pedlars (*smouse*), using horses and carts to transport their merchandise between farms that were frequently many miles apart. They became the bearers of local and even international news to the farmers, as there were few newspapers and no radios or any other form of communication with the outside world.

Percy's grandfather eventually settled in the Swartberg, in the district of Laingsburg. The farmers were very kind and congenial, and he was happy to become accepted as part of the community. He was affectionately known to one and all as 'Oubaas' (a term of endearment which could mean 'Grandpa' but, literally translated, means 'Old Master').

By 1906 he had saved enough money to send for his eldest son, David, who was at a theological college at Telshi, a small town in Lithuania. When he arrived in South Africa David met and fell in love with Esther, a pretty young girl from Johannesburg, but they were soon separated because David went to Stellenbosch to teach biblical Hebrew to the theological students there. (While he was coaching them, they in turn taught him to read and write Afrikaans and English.) After two years he returned to Johannesburg to marry Esther. They decided to settle in Laingsburg because David's father was there, and he encouraged them to take advantage of the ostrich-feather boom in the area. Money was plentiful.

David opened a general store and built a house near it. This became Esther's castle; it never ceased to amaze me how efficiently this young girl from the city kept open house for one and all. She cooked magnificently, and the only acknowledgement she wanted was requests for second and third helpings. (In reality she hated living in Laingsburg, but despite much complaining she remained there for thirty-five years.)

Morris, Percy's older brother, was born twelve years before him, followed by Nancy a few years later. Because of the difference in their ages, initially there was very little contact between the two brothers. While Morris was studying to become a doctor at the University of Cape Town, Percy was at school in the country. Nancy loved both her brothers, and it was she who taught Percy his nursery rhymes and later took pride in his academic and sporting achievements at school and university. This bond between them was very strong and remained so throughout his life.

In the early years the town's activities revolved around the home, the school, sporting activities and the church or synagogue. Although there was a relatively small Jewish community, it was very close-knit. As is the normal custom when a Jewish male reaches the age of thirteen, Percy had to study and read a portion of the law in Hebrew in order to be accepted into the community as an adult. He fell somewhat short of expectations, however, particularly when it came to the customs concerning the dead. A Jewish corpse cannot be left alone; a constant vigil has to be kept until the burial. When Percy, as a so-called adult male, had to act as guard, he described vividly how he shook with fear at the long watch in the dark hours of the night and was as frightened as any normal young boy.

Remembering his youth in Laingsburg, Percy was always very proud of the achievements of the immigrant Jews. So many of them started from humble beginnings. The kindness, hospitality and help of the true Afrikaner was very evident in all small towns. During the Depression in the 1930s there was trust and understanding between Afrikaner and Jew, who helped each other with credit and demanded no payment until things improved.

As a small boy Percy used to be embarrassed by his grandfather, who stood at the window each morning reciting his prayers, with his phylacteries, in true Jewish tradition. He thought that people would mock the old man for his unusual behaviour. Years later he realized that the villagers respected *die Ou Jood* (the Old Jew) for his devout beliefs. He later understood too that it was these same beliefs that helped many of the immigrant Jews to survive. They bought land and built synagogues before they were able to buy their own homes. He said that if he could write, he would tell the story of these wonderful people and call it *They Left No Debts*.

One of Percy's favourite characters in the village was Dassie, who worked as a station porter. He was a simple man who, like members of all the coloured communities at that time, lived in the location, an area set apart from that of the white population. Dassie earned extra money by helping at the local hotel, where he worked on night duty, serving early morning coffee and being of general assistance. No one really knew what Dassie did with his money until many years later, when he invited us to the inaugural service of the church that he had built himself with his lifetime's savings.

Sport played a very important part in the lives of the young people. Percy enjoyed tennis, rugby and, above all else, cricket. He loved to tell the story of the visiting rugby team that came from Sutherland, an even smaller town than theirs, and did not have the added attraction of the railway line passing through it. Laingsburg's rugby field was alongside the railway line, and on one occasion when the home team was unable to penetrate the opposition's forward line and approach their goal, an enterprising member of the team shouted, 'Sutherland, there comes the train!' Sutherland's team became so excited – some of them had never seen a train – that their concentration wavered and Laingsburg rushed in to score.

The first sixteen years of Percy's life passed all too quickly. His desire to become a doctor grew under his brother's influence, as well as that of the local doctor, who frequently allowed Percy to accompany him on his rounds.

After matriculating at Laingsburg, Percy was admitted to the University of Cape Town, where he enrolled as a medical student. Initially he lived at the men's residence, from where he moved to the medical residence. He made friends easily, particularly with those who had also attended schools in country areas. They gained confidence from each other, and in no time they were involved in all the normal fun and games which form such an important part of the life of students, particularly those who are fortunate enough to enjoy the camaraderie of life in residence. He was a conscientious student and was aware of the privilege his father had extended to him by sending him to Cape Town to study.

I met Percy at the beginning of his third-year studies, while I was on a date with his best friend. I soon succumbed to his gentle manner and lovely smile, and we continued to go out with each other until we both qualified. I spent a year at the university before starting to train as a nurse (at that time we were not allowed to begin our training until the age of eighteen). It was generally thought that the only reason I wanted to nurse was to keep an eye on Percy – some price to pay to hold on to a boyfriend!

I loved nursing and still feel that it was one of the most rewarding experiences of my life. Most of my time was spent in children's wards, and I was often involved with children living with various types of cancer. I can vividly remember the sadness, and sometimes despair, that I felt for the patients and parents, and I often wanted to run away from it all, hoping that if I did so, the problems would evaporate into thin air.

In particular one little girl, whom I looked after on night duty, taught me something of great value. This child was so afraid of the unknown that I spent with her every moment I could spare. She told me that she loved me more than the other nurses, and when I asked her the reason she replied, 'When I ask you for cold water, you bring me *cold* water.' What a difference a little piece of ice can make to the happiness of a dying child.

Percy and I grew up together, sharing our laughter and tears, and I think that this was the foundation on which our later life was built. We had the usual courting problems during the ensuing years, but there was never any doubt in our minds that we would get married – and we did, when we had both qualified, in 1947.

We arranged to spend our honeymoon in Port Elizabeth, a nearby seaside resort. It was only after we arrived that I realized that an international cricket test match was scheduled to be played there that week!

Our first years of marriage were not easy for either of us, as we hardly saw each other. Often when one was on night duty the other was working during the day, and incredibly there were times when our paths did not cross for three days at a time – we left little notes for each other. I became aware then that Percy's work was of prime importance in his life.

After completing his one-year housemanship, he worked a further six months in the casualty department of Groote Schuur Hospital. It was during this time that he learned a lesson that subsequently he used many times, with effect, in his lectures to students.

One Saturday afternoon a famous local cricketer was brought into casualty after a match. Percy and a colleague, both equally inexperienced but confident, examined the patient. They organized an x-ray and, on examining the result, they assured the young man that all was well. They told him that he would be able to play the following week. Although he left the hospital in severe pain, the cricketer accepted their diagnosis. His pain persisted and eventually became worse. Finally he consulted an orthopaedic surgeon who diagnosed a fractured thumb, which kept him off the field for a further six weeks.

Seven years later Percy returned to Cape Town as a qualified general surgeon, by now aware that he was very inexperienced and far less confident. One of the first patients whom he was asked to see was the same cricketer's wife. He was thrilled to be called in as a consultant but was anxious that her husband might recognize him and remember the previous diagnosis. This did not happen: the cricketer was much too concerned about his wife's condition. Percy explained that the patient had an obstruction of the bowel and required immediate surgery. The husband agreed, with one proviso – on no account would he allow his wife to be taken to the hospital where he had been treated for his thumb. He explained to Percy, at great length, that he had been completely mismanaged and that he now wanted to make quite sure that no such damned fool as the doctor who had treated him at the time would have anything to do with his wife.

The next two years Percy spent in the state Pathology Department, during which time he decided to make surgery his career. While other young couples went for coffee after a show, we would go to investigate how many cadavers were lined up for the next morning's post-mortems. We decided to go to London, where Percy would study and I would work as a nurse, but our plans were delayed: I became pregnant (the contraceptive pill had yet to be discovered).

I worked in the state Health Department during the first five months of pregnancy but was forced to stop because of severe and persistent nausea. This was the first time that I had experienced discontent, as, apart from feeling ill, I was bored with just being a housewife. Both Percy and I realized, at this early stage of our marriage, how important it is for a wife to be able to pursue interests outside the home; he always advocated that women should either work or participate in other activities that interested them.

Needless to say, he was as thrilled as I was at the birth of our baby daughter, Michele. He had already started studying for the first part of his future examinations, and this, together with his normal work, kept him very busy. Michele became the centre of my life. I treated her like a live doll, even disturbing her sleep to try on her new clothes.

When Michele was eighteen months old we packed our personal belongings and left by ship for London.

Our boat trip on the *Windsor Castle*'s final cruise was a nightmare. Our fares were only £25 per person and £5 per child, so I do not suppose we should have hoped for any sort of luxury. We were packed like sardines in a minute cabin in the bowels of the ship, and there were over a hundred small children on board who were being taken to visit grandparents in Europe for the first time. The food was inedible, which did not worry me: I was far too seasick to care. Percy was all right, as he had an aunt who owned a chocolate business and had sent a gross of chocolate logs down to the ship. He finished them all.

There was a severe outbreak of gastro-enteritis on board, and as the ship's doctor was in a more or less perpetual state of inebriation, there was a continual stream of mothers and children in and out of our small cabin at all times of the day and night. Although he had no medicines or medical equipment with him, Percy was able to reassure the parents – but there was no one to reassure him when Michele developed a very high fever and had a convulsion. This had already happened on a couple of occasions, but Percy had not witnessed it. (Until you see this happen to your own child, you have no idea how frightening it can be.)

We were both relieved to arrive at Southampton. In retrospect, we could not think of one redeeming feature of this trip.

We spent five years in London, which influenced Percy's life greatly. He loved his stay there and had the opportunity to study under some of the most learned doctors and surgeons in the world. Apart from the medical knowledge he acquired, he learned that the most knowledgeable people often show the greatest humility and understanding. He adapted immediately to our new life, which for him was stimulating and exciting, but I was very lonely and unhappy. I hated the small, dingy flats in which we lived, and I worried about our lovely daughter, who was ill for the first eighteen months of our stay. She was in and out of hospital with severe chest infections and never had the beautiful, rosy complexion of the other children.

The everyday things that reduced me to tears then seem very funny now. I used to see the neighbours watching me with amazement as I carried the kitchen chair down to the large coal barrels so that I could lean over to collect the coal from the bottom. It was months later that I discovered small trapdoors underneath for this purpose. The only people who spoke to me were those whom I met at the launderette and the window-cleaner who came once a month. I learned from him that during the first ten months of that year six people in our block had committed suicide. I was not surprised.

My salvation came by the way of a young student from South Africa who came to board with us. Ronnie, who was studying drama at the Royal Academy of Dramatic Art, was seventeen years old. His exuberance and enthusiasm for living were like a breath of sunshine. He was immediately one of the family, and he and Percy became very good friends. We were involved with all his activities, even to the extent of attending the first night of a play in which he had a part. It was in St Martin-in-the-Fields, and Ronnie played a clerk of the court. His part was to bang his gavel and shout, 'Silence in the court!' Percy and I applauded loud and long.

Ronnie endeared himself to the many friends we had now made, mostly doctors and their families who had also come to London to specialize. Thanks largely to his outgoing personality, our parties were always fun. When Percy passed his fellowship examinations Ronnie was the proudest of us all, and this pride was reciprocated tenfold when Ronnie became one of Britain's most famous playwrights and film and television script writers, as well as the publisher of many books. We could not have been more thrilled if he had been our own son.

Although our friends came from all corners of the world, we found that we had a great deal in common. We maintained friendships with many of them; they visited us in South Africa, and we visited them, on many occasions. They became the family we did not have while we were away, and our children have formed friendships with their children and have spent holidays together.

After we had lived in London for a couple of years we took a holiday abroad. I do not think anything could recapture the thrill and excitement of our first visit to France, Switzerland and Italy. We went with our greatest friends, a Canadian couple, and it cost us £100 for the four of us, with all expenses paid, for three weeks. There were times when we could not afford more than a loaf of bread, a piece of cheese and a bottle of wine at the roadside, but these were the memories that remained with us vividly many years later.

At this time Percy became friendly with another Ronald, a prominent surgeon who specialized in cancer treatment. It was he who played a part in influencing Percy to make this study his life's work. Over the following thirty years these two men were in constant contact through their work and friendship.

During our years in London Percy worked very hard and held registrarships at the main teaching hospitals in the fields that particularly interested him. He studied at the same time as he was working, but although his hours were long and arduous, he loved every aspect of London, which remained for him the most 'civilized' part of the world. The only domestic chore I expected him to do was to take Michele out for walks on Sunday mornings so that I could have a couple of hours to myself. After several months Michele complained, however, and I discovered that instead of taking her to the park to feed the ducks, Percy took her to hear 'those funny men shouting from their boxes'! Percy could stand at Hyde Park Corner for hours listening to the speakers.

Apart from his work, which he found stimulating and exciting, he loved all the other things London had to offer. Cricket was his favourite sport both to play and to watch, and through the influence of a friend he even managed to play for a local team. Subsequent trips to London, by some strange coincidence, always seemed to take place just when an important international cricket match was being played at Lord's or the Oval.

Percy enjoyed ballet at Covent Garden, the theatre and television, and he was particularly interested in the politics of the country. Although I shared his interests, I hated the monotony of domestic chores and perhaps resented the pleasure that Percy took in his friends and colleagues. When Michele started to attend a nursery school I decided to take a job, and I employed a sitter, Granny Fisher, to collect her and remain with her until I returned. This proved a great success, as although I paid Granny Fisher my entire salary, Michele loved her, and I found working for a leading West End orthodontist very stimulating.

Life became fun. We bought an old second-hand Austin motorcar, which gave us more pleasure than any other car before or since. It was the type that should have had a running board, but this had been ripped off before purchase, which meant that we had to negotiate a giant step up to the driver's seat. We went on many trips through the beautiful English countryside, and when we visited family staying at the smart Dorchester Hotel, liveried porters always rushed to escort us from our car with umbrellas, in preference to people in their Daimlers and Rolls-Royces. After two years' trouble-free driving we sold our car for the same price as we had paid for it.

My parents visited us on two occasions and spoiled us by taking us on holiday and to lovely restaurants and shows. We realized how much we were all missing by not being together and sharing our experiences. We also became aware that our parents were getting older and were not in the best of health, and this was probably the most important factor in our decision to return to South Africa, which we did in 1955.

Our return trip was certainly the luxury cruise we had dreamed of taking. We travelled on a delightful one-class ship, where we met very congenial people, relaxed on the decks by day and ate, drank and danced through the nights.

When we returned to Cape Town, Percy was very fortunate: he was given a part-time junior consultant's appointment at the Groote Schuur Hospital. He also leased consulting rooms, from where he conducted his private practice. He was lucky too in that his brother Morris, who was a general practitioner, referred as much work to him as possible.

This was a time when the two brothers really got to know each other and learned to respect each other's points of view. At first Percy was still the kid brother, but Morris was quick to appreciate his ability and his concern for his patients, a great bond that they had in common.

One of the most senior surgeons who was in practice welcomed Percy as an assistant, and it was he who instilled confidence in Percy. His honesty and integrity in dealing with people set a wonderful example. We found an apartment, and within six months we once again fitted into a happy routine.

Gillian was born within the first year of our return, and Michele was old enough to adore her baby sister without jealousy. Lawrence was four years younger than Gillian; because of the age difference between them, they were like only children. I used to envy parents who declared that their children loved each other and were good friends. We were always conscious of family loyalty, but the close bond between us became obvious only when Percy fell ill. (It is such a shame that serious problems often have to arise before we are aware of how much we need and depend upon each other. The love and support we all gave and received during Percy's illness were the greatest factors in helping us cope with the situation.)

We had the normal growing pains with all three children, but on the whole we were very fortunate because they accepted the standards that we tried to set for them. Of course we made mistakes, but our children rewarded us by doing their best, and we were proud of them.

Lawrence was a beautiful baby, but unfortunately he developed severe asthma at an early age. I am not sure why I spent those early years trying to underplay his condition and pretend that all was well. Jane, a great friend, put the matter into perspective when she said:

> There was one thing which seemed to be taboo in the Helman home, and that was illness. It was permitted everywhere else but not in their house. I had the impression that if any of Ethel's family was ill, they were actually embarrassed. Every effort was made to ignore the ailment, and it was not the done thing to take any medication or call for assistance from a doctor. Miraculously, they always recovered within a short time.

Once, when Lawrence had a particularly severe attack and had great difficulty in breathing, he became very distressed and asked whether he was going to die. (I think I died a little on that occasion.) I tried to pacify him by telling him not to worry, as his Daddy would soon be home. Between gasps he said, 'I don't want Daddy. I want a proper doctor.'

During these years Percy was working very hard building up a large private practice as well as working on the part-time staff of many hospitals. Fortunately, there was an excellent private nursing home on our doorstep, which was run by nuns, and he performed his private operations there when possible. These admirable women became our very great friends and visited us frequently when they were not on duty. As is often the case with surgeons, work continued through the night as well as at week-ends, and as a result we, as a family, saw very little of Percy. (Lawrence complained that he had never been on a picnic with his family, as all his friends had done. He often amused us with his complaints about us, one of which was that when he was at junior school he was the youngest boy in the class but had the oldest parents.)

As a little girl Gillian shared a room with Lawrence. When he was ill with coughing and vomiting, she would often change his bedding and wash him during the night, and I knew nothing about it until the following morning. She has always been sensitive to the needs of others, just like her father. There was a special bond between them, and I must admit that I often felt a twinge of jealously because of the depth of their feelings towards each other.

Michele has a sunny nature and the gift of self-confidence. She laughs and cries easily, unlike her sister or her father, who felt deeply but rarely allowed himself to show his feelings. I am delighted that she decided to become a nurse. For her too it has been a good choice, as she is compassionate and loves people.

Percy loved having Michele working in the same hospital and often pretended to make passes at her when there were people present who were unaware of the family connection. (He laughingly told the story in reverse: once when he admired a beautiful young nurse in the operating room, she pointedly asked him if he was Michele's father.) He was equally proud of Gillian, who became a doctor and also worked with him. For some reason he was able to show affection more readily to the girls than to Lawrence. Needless to say, he loved his only son dearly, a fact of which I was well aware, but unfortunately neither he nor Lawrence allowed themselves to let down the barriers of their reserve, as they were both very private people.

Percy was an excellent listener and was perceptive about the needs of people with whom he came into contact. As a family man he was interested in all our activities and gave us encouragement and advice at all times.

Lawrence's great love was music, but he refused to have any formal tuition. We and the neighbours suffered agonies as he practised incessantly on the drums, the electric guitar and, eventually, the acoustic guitar. We thought that he sang like an angel. When he and his friends organized a band and performed at a special school concert, we all proudly attended. When Lawrence was due to sing his solo, the bass guitarist turned up the volume on his amplifier and obliterated Lawrence's voice. Percy, who was sitting in the front row, stood up and shouted, much to the amusement of all, 'Spiros, turn down your bass.'

During the time that Percy was building up his professional reputation, I became involved in a crazy business venture. I met Jane, a talented dress designer, and the two of us, with no knowledge or experience but plenty of optimism and enthusiasm, opened a boutique. Our husbands, who were as excited as we were, gave us financial aid and plenty of moral support.

It was very amusing to watch Percy, who had never been aware of ladies' fashions, suddenly become an authority on the subject. There was one memorable occasion when he popped in to see us, as he loved doing whenever he had the time, and we made him remain in the shop while we kept an important appointment across the road. The picture of Percy, sitting at the desk with a huge smile on his face and surrounded by ladies' dresses, will always remain imprinted on my mind.

We led quite a gay social life at this stage. Whenever we attended large functions we used to play a game: we identified the 'Jane Says' dresses worn by the guests, and we compared the number with the 'Percy's operations' present. We ran pretty well neck and neck most of the time, but there was one interesting difference – the ladies paid for their dresses long before they paid for their operations.

These were thirteen wonderful years for us all, and my association with Jane and her husband, Leon, was a rare pleasure, which both Percy and I appreciated enormously. We had fun learning from our mistakes, and our shipper often dined out on some of the outrageous things we unwittingly did.

The time came when Percy did not have the time to spend on his academic work, which he loved. After much discussion and thought, we decided to move from our large house into a small flat, so that Percy could accept a full-time hospital appointment, for this meant a considerable loss of income.

This meant that he could attend many more international conferences and give his research work his undivided attention.

The following three years were the happiest we had experienced, as we had reached a stage of contentment and fulfilment. The two girls had left home – Michele was married at this time, with two lovely boys, and Gillian was completing her medical studies. Lawrence was living with us and studying law at the University of Cape Town. Our flat, overlooking the Atlantic Ocean, was beautifully situated. We had it revamped with the assistance of an enthusiastic and talented young architect, and it became our dream home. Although it was small and unpretentious, we could see the sea from every room including the kitchen, and I embarrassed Percy by boasting that we had the most beautiful home in the world.

Our lifestyle changed considerably. We went for early-morning and late-evening walks, and I enjoyed our companionship and relaxation so much that I retired from work. We really shared our lives for the first time, and Percy even joined in the household chores and the shopping. We went away for weekends, and I managed to persuade him to take an interest in horseracing, which gave us both much pleasure. It really was very funny that Percy, who was very unassuming about all the things about which he was most knowledgeable, should begin to believe that he knew all the answers when it came to horses and bridge, which were by no means his best subjects.

He promised me that I could now join him on all his trips, both local and overseas, and we made plans for his sabbatical leave, a privilege designed to allow people to further their studies for six months away from the hospital. Life was wonderful, and we planned for a wonderful old age together.

Illness 1980–2

For the first time in his life Percy became very ill with infective hepatitis [jaundice]. Coincidentally, a great friend and also a doctor developed the same illness at this time, and we laughingly teased them about this, as the disease can be transmitted by direct contact. Both Percy and Vera were terrible patients. They were not accustomed to being incapacitated, and they both felt very ill indeed. Daily phone calls passed between the two homes comparing signs and symptoms. How yellow were the conjunctivae (eyeballs)? How yellow was the urine? Who felt more nauseous?

The infection lasted three weeks, and in retrospect there are questions about this episode that fill my mind. Was it the beginning of Percy's illness? Would exhaustive tests have revealed any findings? And should Percy have overcome his frustrations and rested until he was really fit? There are no answers, and the ache remains in my heart.

Although he did not feel completely well and still had a raised sedimentation rate (showing that some infection was still present), Percy insisted on going back to work, particularly as he was the secretary organizing an international surgical congress taking place in Cape Town. I was involved in the ladies' committee, and we ourselves left a few days before the end of the meeting to attend another meeting in Monte Carlo.

This was a very special occasion for me, as we planned afterwards to tour America, a country that I had never visited. We were so excited and so rushed before leaving that we both independently forgot to pack our coats.

Percy always participated in the various meetings he attended by reading papers, acting as chairman and taking part in the high-powered discussions. On this trip he made his name for none of the usual reasons.

He always set himself up before the meeting by establishing himself in the front row with his camera and tape-recorder so that he could record and report on all that had taken place on his return home. The members of the various congresses who had not met Percy never knew whether he was a reporter, a photographer or a technician. On this occasion the main projector failed to function during the first lecture. Everyone panicked, and he was urgently called to help them out of their predicament. Nonchalantly he walked up to the machine, gave it a kick and the slides continued to flow. He was the hero of the hour, and *everyone* knew Helman from South Africa after that!

We enjoyed Monte Carlo for its scenic beauty, the interesting people we met and, particularly, the excitement of the casinos. The price of everything was astronomical: it was fortunate that we were there for only a few days.

Washington was one of the most exciting cities we had visited, and Percy spent many hours taking photographs of places of historical interest. We ran from early morning till late at night, and although he always returned to the hotel absolutely exhausted, this did not surprise me. He was still tired each morning, but I took no particular notice; at no stage did he complain to me of not feeling well.

We spent five lovely days at a resort in the Bahamas, where we lazed on the beach, ate luscious meals, met charming people and had a very good rest. We completed our holiday by spending a few days in London to attend shows and visit our favourite haunts. On the plane Percy was not feeling well, but I blamed this on the fact that we had eaten a very inferior Chinese meal the previous night. We had the usual happy home-coming, although one or two people commented that Percy looked rather grey, which we put down to jet lag.

Later Percy was to tell me that at that time he had had premonitions about the seriousness of his condition. Perhaps he said nothing because he was afraid of acknowledging, even to himself, the reality of his vague anxieties. He recorded the following thoughts:

My problem started on an overseas visit – I had been invited to Monte Carlo in April 1980 to attend a very interesting breast cancer conference run by the Johns Hopkins Hospital, Maryland, group. I felt very well and had actually put on some weight.

From Monte Carlo we flew with many of the delegates from America to New York, and from New York we travelled and had a marvellous holiday in America. We visited Washington, Las Vegas, where we spent a lot of time in the casinos. We went downtown, visiting the Strip, saw a lot of shows, running all over the place, and just having a wonderful time. From there we went to San Francisco and then to Los Angeles, and on to a lovely hotel, the Fontainebleau, in Miami. In the Bahamas we met some most interesting people.

On this trip I became aware of cramps after meals. I had ascribed these symptoms, which I'd never had before, to the food I'd been eating and tried to change the food. The cramps persisted, although not very bad at the time.

During the course of the holiday I became aware of a swelling in the right upper quadrant of my abdomen, and I knew I was in for a lot of trouble. I was shaken by this lump, although it was quite painless, and I wondered whether we should cut short our holiday and return to Cape Town. As we only had another two or three weeks to go I decided to complete our holiday as planned.

When I returned at the beginning of June, my appetite had dropped and I was having a fair amount of cramps after meals, and was aware that the lump was getting bigger.

On our return home there was an urgent message from Morris to contact him immediately. The call concerned a woman with a breast problem who had been awaiting Percy's return, and after consultation he arranged to operate on her the following day. This emergency, together with his other work, did not give him much time to ponder upon his own worries.

After supper that night we decided to take a short walk along the sea front. It was a beautiful evening, the air balmy and cool.

We walked some short distance without speaking, then I happened to glance at Percy and noticed that his face looked tired and drawn in the twilight. He stopped, clutched himself and groaned. I was most alarmed and insisted we return to the flat immediately. Once we were indoors the pain subsided, but he told me, without emotion, that he had arranged to have a barium enema the following day. This is Percy's account of what happened:

I went to see Ronnie and asked him to arrange for me to have a barium enema. I had no other symptoms apart from the cramps after meals and some pain in the right upper side of my abdomen. My bowels were regular and with the loss of appetite I had lost about five kilos in weight. I was feeling reasonably well.

Now, I had sent many people to have barium enemas, but I never knew just how uncomfortable the procedure was. First of all you are dressed in an awful back-to-front cotton dressing-gown. You have to lie on a very cold x-ray table with a machine pointing at you at very close range. The insertion of the dye rectally was uncomfortable, and even more uncomfortable was the change of posture. You are told to turn to the left, then to the right and it felt that the air was sort of bursting your abdomen. It's just one of those things, I suppose – that is how a barium enema is done!

When I got dressed after the enema, Ronnie, with a very sad expression told me that I had carcinoma of the right half of the transverse colon. There was a typical apple-core lesion, and there was a considerable amount of narrowing of the bowel. He patted me on the back, and gave me the x-rays and said how sorry he was.

You can imagine my state of anguish, although I had expected something like this. I took these pictures unbelievingly, and, sick with worry, I walked down the long F floor corridor of the outpatients where the x-rays were done. I walked outside the hospital, through the main entrance, past ward A1, not knowing where to go. I bumped into one of the physicians who said in his usual cheerful way, 'How are you?' I suppose he couldn't understand my expression when I answered, 'Only fair' – and walked off.

I was in a tremendous dilemma because I didn't know whom I

should ask to operate on me. There were about four or five surgeons I could have easily chosen.

Although I knew that Percy was going to have the barium enema, I did not even suggest accompanying him, as I did not believe that his symptoms were ominous. He promised that he would phone me as soon as he got the results, so I stayed home waiting for the call.

At ten o'clock in the morning the phone rang, and Percy, in a perfectly controlled voice, told me that he had a malignant lesion of the colon. I now know what a state of shock means, as I was completely stunned and could not believe him. I did not hear a single word he said after that initial statement. I must have answered but have no recollection of what I said. He put down the phone at his end, and I sat in a completely dazed condition, without moving, for at least half an hour.

The tape continues:

Ethel actually suggested that we should go overseas to see some expert men, but that I was totally against. I knew that I wanted to be at Groote Schuur Hospital, in a ward where I knew everyone and where everyone knew me. I chose David because he was an excellent surgeon, and I knew that I would get the very best attention possible. I showed David the x-rays.

David recalls the morning on which Percy came to see him, carrying some x-rays.

Percy: David, have you a moment to look at these x-rays with me?
David: Sure, Percy. What have you got there? Something interesting?
Percy: This plate.
David: Oh, yes. There it is. Transverse colon. The crab [term for cancer]. Quite a big one.
Percy: These are my own x-rays.

In this life there are those rare moments when one is talking to an individual who is totally exposed, vulnerable, open. Percy was then. A man standing with his death sentence in his hand, rather than an internationally known cancer surgeon. He was open, vulnerable, but in quiet control of the situation.

David: Percy, I'm sorry. It looks quite a large one . . .
Percy: It will have to come out, of course. Would you be kind enough to do the operation?
David: Of course, of course. As soon as possible. When can you come in? Can you come in tomorrow?
Percy: Whenever it is convenient and whenever it suits you.

Later, David was to write:

It is flattering for an architect to have another ask him to design his house, so too for a doctor to have another seek his help, and the more so for a surgeon consulted by a colleague. It is overwhelming when a cancer specialist asks one to remove his own cancer, especially when he is one's teacher in surgical training. A man whose professional life has been the study of cancer. Someone who has been fascinated by cause, growth, diagnosis, spread, survival. Someone who has been trying to understand the special malevolence of the malignant cell. Someone on whom the malignant cell has viciously turned. This was not flattering; it was overwhelming.

The initial shock of learning that you have cancer is probably one of the worst experiences an individual can suffer. Percy described it later as 'the worst sort of nightmare, as if there is an explosion in your head'. In a lecture he subsequently gave, entitled 'Thoughts in the Mind of a Patient Living with Cancer', he described the initial shock as being 'so severe that although you hear the words, they do not really penetrate the consciousness'.

The children were equally shocked and were unable to grasp the position. When I phoned Michele she realized from my tone of voice that all was not well. She knew that her father was due to undergo investigations, and when I told her that the barium enema had confirmed a tumour she just put the phone down. She did not ask where the tumour was or whether it was malignant. She felt as if the whole world was crashing down around her. Later that day she explained that she could not even phone her husband but just sat in her lounge, her thoughts going over her whole life at home with us, and as a married woman, up to this moment. It seemed to her like some kind of nightmare that could not possibly be happening to her. She felt that her early life had been perfect; nothing had ever gone wrong; the bad things always happened to other people. She kept wanting to put the clock back, even just twenty-four hours. She knew, as a nursing sister, what the future held, and at this stage she did not know if she was strong enough to cope with the situation. Until then Michele had felt that I was the pillar of strength on which they could depend, and she hoped that she would now be able to support us.

That afternoon she picked up the phone to speak to Percy. She lifted and replaced the receiver a number of times, unable to control her tears. She did not want him to hear her crying, as she wanted to give him strength. At last she managed to get through and she heard him say, 'My darling, if I could do something about it, I would but there is nothing I can do.'

Gillian had recently married, and both she and her husband Jeff were working as housemen at the hospital. Percy phoned Jeff and asked him to tell Gillian about his diagnosis. Her first reaction to her husband's call was stunned disbelief, followed by shock and tears. When she phoned Percy he told her that the lesion was palpable (it could be felt). She knew the significance of this and shouted back at him, '*Palpable*!', realizing that this meant that he had a very late and large lesion. Poor Gillian – she later confided that she had walked around the rest of that day in alternate states of hope and despair. She hoped that the disease would be confined and worried that it would be too widespread. She made a pretence of carrying on with her work but was unable to concentrate.

When Lawrence returned from university and we told him the news, he just stood in shocked silence. He described his feelings at a later stage.

Cancer came up often in our conversation at home. It was not unusual to bring it up at the dinner table. Cancer was, in a sense, my father's job. I became quite familiar with the terminology at an early age. From ten onwards I have been taking detailed telephone messages from the registrars and housemen (who regularly overlooked the fact that not every youngster was trained in the jargon of medical science), concerning diagnosis and progress of my father's patients. I soon learned to tell the difference between good news and bad, and when I heard that it was a carcinoma of the colon I knew what to expect.

That night we made no attempt to sleep. We were like drowning people in an ocean of turbulent water. We discussed every angle of his illness and the best and worst possibilities. There was the hollow hope that the diagnosis was incorrect or that the tumour could be completely removed surgically. And there was the possibility of widespread disease and a limited lifespan. We understood, for the first time, just how precious life is, and we clung to each other as if we had been thrown a life-line. We cried until we had no tears left, and we made a vow that we would maintain complete trust and honesty so that we could face together whatever lay ahead.

It is not easy to assess the worst part of any bad situation, but I feel that when a patient realizes he has cancer, he dies a little at this stage. Regardless of whether he recovers completely or not, that shock and despair cannot be obliterated from his mind. It is my belief that if the feeling of helplessness can gradually be overcome and the position accepted, then the other things will automatically fall into place. Some people take longer than others to adjust, and unfortunately there are those who are never able to do so, but I do believe that patience, tolerance, great gentleness and a deep feeling of loving care can help as much as any medication. It was these principles, and the firm decision not to let either partner feel alone, that enabled us to become aware of how wonderful it is to share life to the full.

When we discussed the utter despair we both experienced that night, we realized just how much we loved and needed each other. It was as if a small flame had caught alight; it gave us the comfort of a warm, crackling fire on a cold night.

5–19 June 1980

The next morning, 5 June, I accompanied Percy to the hospital, where the admission clerk remarked on how dashing he looked in his new hat, which he had purchased in the South of France. The sister and staff were so kind and friendly that I understood just why Percy wanted to be at Groote Schuur Hospital. The day actually passed quite pleasantly, with people popping in and out.

Percy recorded his reaction to his arrival at the hospital, this time as a patient:

> I found myself in a rather luxurious room, a double-bedded ward from which one bed had been removed to accommodate a couple of comfortable chairs. They had installed a telephone and had everything prepared for my comfort and convenience.

The sister in charge of the ward was aware of how important it would be for me to be involved actively in caring for Percy, so she allowed me to assist in his nursing.

The morning of 6 June I arrived at the hospital early to help prepare him for the operation. This involved washing and shaving the whole area of the abdomen and genitalia, cleaning the skin with a special solution and dressing him in an operation gown and boots. As Percy was a very shy person, he was happy for me to do these personal things for him; my involvement that morning set the pattern for the following weeks. We were not as tense as before. We actually joked while the preparations were taking place, as we felt as if we were on a treadmill that was already in motion, and there was no stepping off.

These were Percy's impressions of the next stage:

> Firstly, I never realized how narrow that operating table was, and I thought I was going to fall off the damn thing. Although I

was very drowsy, I still thought I was going to fall off. I remember how happy I was to see Sister Olivier, my favourite operating sister, taking the case. I was confident at the sight of Sister Jurgens hovering over me, making me as comfortable as possible, and the quiet efficiency of Gay giving the anaesthetic.

The operation seemed to last for ever. Percy's brother Morris and his sister Nancy, Michele, a friend and I waited in the ward, where the tension was palpable. There were periods of complete silence and others when everyone spoke together. The nurses brought innumerable cups of tea, most of which were left untouched. The very fact that they brought the tea made us aware of how concerned they all were. Behind the closed doors the operation proceeded.

After what seemed an eternity David, the surgeon, walked in and told us that all was not well. He had found a large, malignant tumour, indicating that the cancer had reached an advanced state. We were speechless. By this time Gillian had arrived to hear the sad news. What started off as a quiet state of shock ended up with us all screaming at each other. Our nerves were stretched to breaking point, and we started to discuss what we were going to tell Percy.

Michele (a trained nurse) and Gillian (a doctor) thought that we should tell him the whole truth immediately. I felt that we should await the right time. Morris (a general practitioner) did not want him told at all. My feelings were that every patient has the right to be told the truth about his condition, but I have always felt that timing for this was of the utmost importance. I believe that most patients who have cancer know of their condition. People lose respect for those caring for them when they perceive that they are not being told the truth, but one's words must be carefully chosen at a suitable stage.

In the intensive-care unit Percy rose to consciousness, opened his eyes, smiled and then slept again, as if he were on a see-saw. He was kept sedated day and night during the first few days, and the waves of acute pain were counteracted by sleep. He recalled later:

I woke up in the intensive-care ward with excruciating abdominal pain. They had ordered monitoring with morphine for the pain, but in the busy intensive-care unit this is not always possible when the sisters are so busy. The sister will give morphine intravenously and then disappear. What you really need is to actually have someone sitting with you, monitoring the pain and giving the drugs as required. If this is not possible, I would have preferred for my patients and myself to have the drugs given over regular intervals before the pain became severe. Apart from the pain I was obsessed by the fact that I might not be able to pass urine, and I was determined not to have a catheter passed. I got out of bed even about six hours after the operation to pass water and was fortunate in being able to do so regularly.

The girls in the intensive-care unit were excellent, looking after me very well. The tube into my stomach was a damn nuisance, but the drip into my arm was not so bad. After twenty-four or forty-eight hours I was shifted to my ward again, and I felt a lot more comfortable. After about three days I was relieved to have the Ryle's [nasogastric] tube removed.

When all the caring family had returned home I remember looking out of the window of the hospital ward and wondering how it was possible that everything looked the same. Why hadn't the traffic drawn to a halt? Why hadn't the sun stopped shining? How was it possible that everyone could not see how much I was suffering? I felt a strange sense of unreality about my surroundings and became aware for the first time of how I had previously accepted good health as our due, instead of appreciating it as the most precious gift on earth.

Those first few nights, as I lay alone in our double-bed, the craziest thoughts rushed through my mind. I willed Percy's disease to be transferred to me, as I felt that it would be easier that way. I wished that his cancer would be contagious, so that we could go through it together, like two children with measles. I longed to be able to help him with my health and strength and to ease the burden of his suffering. The thought that was uppermost in my mind was that we should be able to share the pain as we had shared the good things in life.

When friends had experienced such problems I had wondered how they survived, not realizing that there is no choice. In retrospect I think that this time is of primary importance to the patient as well as to family and friends. Gentleness and loving care can perhaps ease the desolation and loneliness that the patient invariably suffers. Percy himself described the feeling of togetherness that helped him cope with the situation:

> The greatest comfort of all is having an understanding family. This was the time beyond all others that I realized how much I loved and needed my wife. She had an iron steadfastness and courage, and there was a fathomless emotion which enabled us to face things together.

As is often the case with doctors, Percy developed complications. Five days after the operation he was in great pain, became cold and clammy and was convinced that the wound had opened:

> I had tremendous pain and there was some bleeding from the drain site. I had visions of the anastomosis parting and called for David. He came immediately and looked a bit worried but behaved as if there was nothing serious wrong. They packed and repacked the area, and fortunately the bleeding stopped.

In fact it was not all that serious, but at the time we were abnormally worried.

Normally three or four days after an abdominal operation the patient is able to pass wind, which is an indication that the tube into the stomach can be removed. After ten days this still had not taken place; Percy had a distended abdomen, which was most uncomfortable and caused concern. David called in Bill, a colleague and friend, to discuss further treatment, and they decided to re-operate. Percy solved the problem his own way, however:

> My problem was that I had a tremendous ileus [temporary paralysis of the bowel], and by the tenth postoperative day I still

had not passed flatus. I had a blown abdomen and I had vomited. I was still on a drip and Bill was consulted. An x-ray showed a couple of fluid levels, but I did not have abdominal pain. I remember how distressed I was when they said they had to re-operate. I got such a fright that I passed flatus at that moment . . . and after a gentle enema given by Ethel, I had a tremendous bowel action. I was free of all discomfort and my ileus was finished, over, and I was ready to go home.

In between these two events, Percy suffered from severe hic-coughing, which continued unabated for nearly five days. Not only was it distressing for Percy, but it was uncomfortable for all of us who witnessed it. He was particularly upset as he remem-bered that both his father and grandfather had severe hiccoughs before they died.

The doctors tried all the normal medication to stop the spasm and even reverted to old wives' tales but with no success. Continuous sedation controlled the hiccoughs to some extent, and sleep relieved him slightly. The doctors and nurses suggested that he be kept as quiet as possible and no visitors were allowed. Even the opening of the door would be enough to set him off, so I sat like a sentry on a bench outside, preventing anyone from entering. I was like one possessed and carried out every instruction to the letter. When I even refused to let Morris in to see Percy, when he had taken the afternoon off from his busy practice to be with his brother, he was very annoyed with me.

I thought of nothing but Percy and his welfare. If the whole world had exploded around me at that time, I don't think I would have been aware of it. I was always gentle and sympathetic with him, but I needed to devote to him every bit of feeling I possessed, and as a result I neglected other people's concern for him.

My friends told me that at the onset of Percy's illness I became brittle and unapproachable, and they felt that if they put a foot wrong, I would probably snap and the whole façade I had created would crumble. Apparently my attitude was: 'Percy is going to be fine.' The fact that I was actively able to nurse and care for him probably helped me more than it helped Percy. It is so important to members of families and friends to be able to do something for the patient, even if it is sitting quietly and holding his hand.

In the beginning he never inquired about the findings at the time of the operation. He must have suspected that all was not well because had the prognosis been good, we would have all rushed to tell him the good news. The patient needs to feel the support and comfort of the person who is giving him the worst news of his life. One might argue that the right moment never comes, but a sensitive doctor or family knows instinctively when the time is right. Once everything is brought out into the open, the patient invariably feels that a great burden has been removed. I sensed that Percy did not want to hear the full implications of his situation immediately but needed time to adjust to the circumstances.

On the fifth day after the operation David discussed the findings with Percy. The conversation went like this:

Percy: David, have you had the pathology back yet?
David: No, but perhaps we should have a talk. You see, Percy, there was peritoneal involvement. You and I don't want to hide anything. There was some involvement.
Percy: Involvement? Yes, I see. I fully understand. Yes. Thank you. You will understand that I have to organize my situation. Yes. Thank you. You have been really marvellous about everything. Thank you. I couldn't have had anyone better to look after me . . . Did you say peritoneal involvement? How long do you think I will be in hospital – I mean now?

Later Percy recorded his immediate reaction to this news:

The shock, of course, came the next day, when David told me that the growth was large and that it had penetrated the serosa [covering of the gut], that nodes [lymph glands] were involved and that I had peritoneal seedlings. I had great difficulty in reconciling myself to the situation. This thing shook me. It was hard to believe because at the age of fifty-six I was feeling so well, and I thought that I was quite indestructible. I knew the situation was very serious, and I expected the worst.

Percy's surgeon, David, was extremely kind and receptive to me at all times, and, apart from being grateful to him for his superb handling of Percy, I always felt that I could approach David with anything that was worrying me, however unimportant. When he discussed the possibility of chemotherapy (drug treatment) and irradiation (radiotherapy) after the operation, I was fully prepared to take Percy overseas, where I imagined that there might be more advanced methods. At this stage I had not met the doctor who was to treat Percy, but when I did so subsequently I, like Percy, was perfectly confident that he could not receive better or more care anywhere in the world. David explained:

> The current practice is for surgeons to perform their cancer operations and then refer their patients to an oncologist for additional chemotherapy and irradiation. The decision in Percy's case was not an easy one. I personally had a rather strong, if not an over-reactive, view about this treatment, and so did Percy himself. But Percy made my decision easier. 'I'm in your hands,' he said, 'and you must do what you think best.' So, after a number of international phone calls and consultation with senior colleagues, in particular 'senior statesman' Bill, I referred Percy to the oncologists. [Oncologist describes a physician who specialises in non-surgical treatment of cancer.]

Dudley was the chosen oncologist:

> In June of 1980 I was very saddened and distressed to hear that Percy Helman, senior surgeon at Groote Schuur Hospital, had undergone surgery for bowel cancer. My first reaction was that of shock and despair, as here was an individual who knew so much about malignancy and who for so long had dedicated a great deal of his professional career to the treatment of this disease and must now face the impact his condition would have on him and his family. I wondered how he would react to his diagnosis, how much his surgeon would tell him regarding the extent of his

disease and if he would request postoperative therapy. And, most important of all, would he be able to accept and cope psychologically? Percy knew I had been requested to see him and was very pleased to see me. This put me at ease immediately, and after a while, after the initial tension had worn off, he told me that he would accept any form of treatment that I would deem necessary. This was, to me, a most humbling gesture, as I realized that he had given the whole matter of future treatment a great deal of thought and was now placing his trust in somebody who had been his student.

(It was agreed that treatment using 5-fluorouracil (5FU) would start just before he left hospital and would be continued at home.)

The day after Percy had the bowel action he started feeling much better, and there was talk of his coming home.

One of the most important factors in his recovery from his operation, apart from surgical procedures, was the excellent way in which his colleagues dealt with him, and I think that this is an important lesson for us all. At no time was Percy made to feel a 'lesser' person. On the contrary, after meetings that were of particular interest to him, his friends used to come to his ward, discuss the proceedings with him and ask his advice. This was always done with the greatest consideration and tact, and they were fully aware of just how much could be discussed without over-taxing his strength. The doctors involved were David, John (the professor in charge of the whole surgical department) and his great friend and colleague, Bill. They were all outstanding men. Bill, a very special person of great experience and empathy, immediately told Percy to prepare his lecture for the Journal Club, which was due to take place within a few weeks. At the time I was speechless at this suggestion and only later realized that it had been planned with great thought and foresight. Percy at first refused, saying he would never be up to it, but Bill gave him a friendly nudge, and said, 'What on earth do you think you will do when you get home? You will have all the time in the world!'

The question of feeling a 'lesser' person is a very real one for seriously ill patients. Apart from the loss of dignity that is a natural consequence of dependency on others, there is an inescapable feeling that because health and strength have disappeared, the image that others have of them, which is all-important, has somehow diminished as well. It is difficult for a healthy person to appreciate these feelings. Often those in attendance will misinterpret the patient's diffident remarks about being 'useless' as simply the product of self-pity, but these feelings go much deeper. We all rely on an image of ourselves – strong, healthy, confident, self-assured, whatever it might be – that good health gives us, but confidence quickly evaporates when circumstances change and a formerly strong person becomes weak and frail. If recovery is not far off, the feeling may be only temporary, but in the terminally ill it will persist and grow, and the patient may sink into deep depression if not encouraged somehow to ignore as far as possible the physical illness and to concentrate on the spiritual and mental attributes that he or she still possesses.

Fortunately for us all, Percy had a vast store of inner resources to call on, and his personality developed more fully through his sufferings. And the strong, healthy people who attended him learned a great deal too from his humility, his capacity for endurance and his will to go on living. He seemed to grow in stature through his experience and we all enjoyed being with him.

Visitors can be of very great importance to the patient, as was the case with Percy. The matter of visitors needs to be handled prudently, as very often they are more aware of their own needs than those of the patient. There were times when Percy loved seeing people and others when he yearned for solitude. When he was feeling nauseous and suffering from continuous hiccoughing he did not wish to see anyone, including close family, as he was aware of how distressing the situation was to others as well as to himself. He mentioned later that as a doctor he often used to

drop in to see a patient with whom he was friendly on his way to
or from a ward round. At the time he did not realize how
inconvenient it may have been to the patient, who probably
received half a dozen visits from doctors daily. If the patient feels
well he probably enjoys the diversion, but if not, visitors can be
very exhausting. Percy described his feelings thus:

> I can remember the visitors who came to see me after my first
> operation and those who did not come at all. I suppose I under-
> stand because they couldn't face me. There were those who came
> carrying bunches of flowers and presents, rushing into the room
> saying how marvellous I looked when I knew I was looking like
> all hell. I was in fact feeling terrible, green and nauseous, with an
> ileus and wanting to vomit. These people were quite offensive to
> me, and I felt that I couldn't believe anything they had to say. The
> third lot I appreciated most of all. They just sat down and held my
> hand and said, 'Percy, I don't know what to say to you.' And they
> sat quietly and we contemplated the whole situation.

The support of the people with whom he worked and the
interest they showed helped him tremendously:

> John came to see me daily and told me that I didn't need to worry
> about work. He told me to do as much as I wanted to do, and no
> matter what, he would see to it that my post would be kept in
> order. His comfort was of immense value to me and bucked me
> up no end.

The medical superintendent and the dean of the university were
also most supportive.

> This was all most reassuring and a tremendous emotional experi-
> ence, and when people of this calibre behaved in this way I cried
> unashamedly, very often because of their very kindness.

20 June – 31 August 1980

The cold facts of a hospital file in no way indicate the underlying emotions involved. Percy's read baldly:

ADMITTED   5.6.1980 to Ward B1
OPERATION   6.6.1980
DISCHARGED   19.6.1980

but those two weeks were a lifetime of experiences that affected many people. For Percy and for us it was a time of adjustment to a different concept of life.

There are no hard-and-fast rules concerning cancer. The patient may well be completely cured. No one can change the physical process of the disease, but I honestly believe that a positive mental attitude can improve the quality and even the quantity of life. This obviously takes time and effort on the part of the patient and all those involved with him, but it is very important that there should always be hope and belief in the future. Percy himself stated:

> The doctor should be honest at all times with the patient and encourage him to talk about his fears and worries, however trivial they may seem. There must be a basic confidence between the doctor and patient, and stress must be put on the unpredictability of cancer. Even when problems arise, there should always be a sense of hope. Where all treatment is concerned the doctor should show concern and compassion, and humility is always a good starting point . . . patients can live well for many years, even with metastases [recurrence of the disease] and often might die from an entirely different cause. So many of these patients outlive their doctors and are able to lead a full and productive life.

Two weeks after Percy's admission to hospital he was allowed to go home, and I remember how thrilled I was at the prospect. I arrived with a large parcel of brand-new clothes, as I did not want his weight loss to be obvious. He had tears in his eyes when he tried them on but ended up by laughing heartily: instead of buying trousers one size smaller than usual, I should have bought one size larger. Even his regular trousers would not meet

around his waist (his abdomen would have been swollen whatever the operation). Percy left in his dressing-gown, delighted to
be going home.

We had made the journey from the hospital many times
before, but on this occasion both of us were so emotional that
neither could utter a word. The whole landscape was different,
as though we were seeing it for the first or the last time. We were
afraid of what the future had in store for us. Was Percy going to
die? How long might he live? What sort of life would we lead?
How and when would the end come? We were both quiet with
our own thoughts.

We entered the flat, where Lawrence was waiting for us. We
all hugged each other and shed a few tears but did not talk much.
In a way we had left our son Lawrence out of the whole
situation, as we had wrongly decided to try to shield him from
our problems. He was twenty years old, not completely adult but
certainly not a child. By excluding him from our suffering we did
him an injustice. Percy's minor obsession was that nothing
should interfere with Lawrence's studies; he felt that if he did not
discuss the seriousness of his condition with Lawrence, his son
would be unaware of the position. This was obviously a mistake,
as Lawrence is an intelligent, sensitive person, and he was aware,
instinctively, of everything we tried to hide. His suffering must
have been even worse than ours because we shared our feelings,
and any experience shared, however bad, is better than being
excluded.

The girls were beside themselves with worry and distress, but
they had their own lives to lead and were not closeted in a small
flat with people continually coming and going and the phone
ringing incessantly. Lawrence, on the other hand, was expected
to carry on a normal life and continue studying as if everything
were just as it had always been. We should all have sat down
together and debated the matter sensibly. We should have given
Lawrence the choice of remaining with us or perhaps moving in
with Michele for a while. I was obsessed with Percy's welfare
and was perhaps insensitive to other people's feelings, particularly
Lawrence's. Fortunately, this problem was eventually discussed

and brought into the open, but not before great heartache had been suffered by us all.

One Friday evening, which has always been family night to celebrate the Sabbath, Percy was in the middle of a course of treatment and feeling very unwell. Lawrence walked into the flat late and did not greet Percy particularly warmly. For the first and only time Percy completely lost control of his emotions and accused Lawrence of having no feeling for him whatsoever, after which he left the table and refused to continue with the dinner. I followed him to the bedroom, where I found him sobbing in a chair. Apart from feeling ill and depressed, he felt that Lawrence had rejected him. I was torn between the two of them: I knew that Percy was being unreasonable, but it took time to persuade Lawrence to apologize to his father because Lawrence himself was hurt that Percy should ever have doubted his concern. As he wrote subsequently:

> During the period of his illness I was aware of the tremendous effort my father was making to carry on as normal. There were times when he came home from work looking tired and depressed, and I noticed how he avoided doing anything which may have reminded him of his illness. I had decided from the outset to behave as if nothing had happened and I fear that he interpreted this as an uncaring attitude.

This memory is still painful to me long after the event. I now believe that we cannot bear our children's pain and grief for them, however young or old they are. Even young children should be encouraged to share in pain or grief according to their limitations.

Those first few weeks after Percy came home from hospital passed quite uneventfully. We all took care that Percy was in no way overstressed by physical exertion or by receiving too many visitors. Apart from sleeping for short periods during the day, with mild sedation he slept very well at night. I found the nights the greatest strain, as I rarely slept for more than a few hours. I used to watch Percy from my side of the bed and felt that he was slipping through my fingers. I saw him as if I were looking through the wrong end of a telescope, as if he were moving further and further away. I used to wake with a start and pray that it was all a ghastly nightmare. On one occasion I woke with real tears streaming down my cheeks, as I had dreamed that Percy was dead. I had to take myself firmly in hand and put an end to these fantasies. Percy was not dead; he was very much alive and lying next to me, and he was getting stronger every day. I decided at this point that it was important to enjoy every moment we had together, to live for the present and let the future care for itself. Percy's reaction seems to have been similar:

> When I left hospital I realized the sudden change in my whole situation. In my work one of the most difficult things was that I was unable to plan for the future. I had received many invitations to attend congresses and to visit people. Invitations were coming in for my going to Berne, Lausanne and London in December, also for August and November of next year, and I thought at the time that it was impossible to plan and make arrangements. But it is strange how one reacts to these things, as you somehow do accept invitations and so make arrangements and sort of go along as if things are going to be all right.

Dudley, who is an extremely compassionate doctor, was aware that Percy was concerned that he needed treatment. He was given cytotoxic therapy (the injection of anti-cancer drugs into a vein) to allay the growth of the cancer cells. In order to make life easier for Percy, Dudley came to the flat himself daily for three days after the first two doses of the first course had been given in hospital.

According to the doctors, Percy's reaction to the treatment was normal, but for the patient it was a very difficult period. He developed sores and blotches on his face and scalp at first and complained of feeling very lethargic. On tape he described how he felt:

> Dudley was absolutely magnificent, and he would come to my flat and give me 5-fluorouracil 5FU (the drug being used) daily for

five days every month. These drugs affected me quite severely. I felt 'pap' and it affected my hair – not that I had much. Dudley subsequently told me that I needed x-ray therapy, and this was another terrible experience. You had to go every morning and lie on a hard table, a lonely person in a room with this huge machine hovering over you making a sort of peculiar hurrying, splashing noise as it finished. The treatment only lasted about a minute or two at a time, and the girls looking after me were marvellous, always kind but firm.

I believe that the thoughts underlying the treatment were what was worrying Percy. As is often the case with doctors, he could only think of the worst prognosis when it came to himself. His distress obviously affected me, and when I saw the area they had marked off on his body with a dark-blue pen I wanted to cry out loud. At a later stage we both realized how stupid our reactions had been, but it is difficult to be logical at times of extreme mental distress. I tried to make light of the fact that he had to be bed-bathed at this stage because the areas that were being irradiated were not allowed to get wet, but I was fully aware of his own sense of inadequacy. It is the little things that often harass the patient far more than severe problems.

Help came too from another quarter. Our friend from London wrote regularly, advising on treatment and suggesting beneficial foods: plenty of fresh fruit juice, fresh vegetables (particularly carrots) and light, nutritious meals. Diet is important at all stages of convalescence, but the patient must be encouraged to eat the necessary foods in a very diplomatic way. At no stage should eating become a fetish, but small, tempting meals should be presented. Always give the patient a little less than you think he can manage, as he gets great satisfaction from finishing what is on his plate. Percy was very co-operative and enjoyed the fun we had in preparing things:

Ethel saw to it that I ate all the best foods that I could possibly have and implored me to eat. Got all sorts of things, fresh orange juice, strawberries and the best of everything. I think that it was her doing that kept me going and kept my strength going.

Living with cancer requires many compromises, particularly while the patient is having treatment. He tires easily; he has no energy; and he becomes depressed. It is important to plan your life accordingly. The first priority is to let the patient do as much or as little as he wishes. Some people want to work and carry on as normally as possible; others do not feel up to it. I feel strongly that nothing should be forced on to the patient and that he should be allowed to adjust to his own tempo. Quality of life is all-important. If it is work that adds to this, then encourage the patient to do as much as possible, and if he only wants to rest, do not make him feel guilty about that. I do think that this is one time when the patient should be indulged like a small child. Even self-pity is acceptable at this stage, as no one who has not experienced serious illness can know what the patient is suffering, mentally as well as physically. Fortunately, this is usually only a temporary phase, and in Percy's case he slept a great deal of the time – perhaps sleep was his own defence mechanism.

From our experience I think it is a good idea to set goals day by day. When Percy first returned from hospital he did not dress for the first few days but sat in a chair in his dressing-gown for a couple of hours in the morning and afternoon. He loved visitors but found that he quickly got tired if he talked to too many people at one time, so we staggered the callers. Little things like taking a bath, shaving and getting dressed all became milestones. When you are well you take such things for granted, but it is quite remarkable how priorities change when you become seriously ill. I vividly remember the occasion when Percy first crossed the road in front of our flat to sit on the bench facing the sea – it was as if he had won a marathon.

We all had to adjust to the change of circumstances, but the example set by Percy was exceptional, and we did our best to try to follow it. At no stage did he ask, 'Why me?', often the question that is uppermost in the mind of the patient. I asked him about this, and he explained that being a doctor and a scientist had made him very aware of the fact that tragedy strikes indiscriminately at any time and that he was no different from others. He confessed that he was puzzled by one thing, however: he could not understand why he was singled out for the love, respect and acclaim of the many people around him. My sincere answer was that he was the sort of man everyone would like to emulate, a caring, thoroughly honest and decent human being.

As if to prove my point, Percy received many cards and letters wishing him well. In particular, one from an older and much respected colleague, who also had carcinoma of the colon, amazed and delighted him and provoked a strong emotional response in him. It read:

Dear Percy

I was shocked when I learned of your plight. And I felt that as a fellow sufferer and friend, I must write to you. Because I think I know how you must feel, how difficult it is to be courageous in times of depression. How, when one feels that one has come to terms with oneself, one receives kindness from friends and from unsuspected quarters, one is plunged again into a period of sadness. I prefer to think that these moments of sadness are not moments of self-pity.

It must be inevitable that you will be taking stock of things, and what you have achieved in your years of endeavour. And I guess, you have more than a share of regrets and bothers. I don't think that you have any cause of these. The balance sheet is clearly in the black. Whatever it has been, looking after students and patients, or your relationship with your colleagues, you have really set a standard to which few can measure.

The letter continued to praise Percy and to give him encouragement, but its greatest value lay in the fact that someone else knew exactly how he was feeling.

'Kindness from unsuspected quarters' is what brought tears to our eyes on several occasions. We were moved by the ward orderly who repeatedly stood outside Percy's door waiting for the 'No Visitors' notice to be removed so that he could walk in and shake him by the hand without saying a word; by our cleaning lady who had difficulty in reading and writing but still managed to leave little notes telling us how much she cared; by my sympathetic hairdresser who was only waiting to hear when Percy started to give me cheek (when I reported that he had reprimanded me for using his best imported sherry for making a trifle for supper, she immediately sent her busy shampooist to her flat to get her husband's half-bottle of Bristol Cream, which she sent to Percy with her love); by friends who went to great lengths to find out what Percy's favourite foods were and stocked our fridge with chicken soup (Jewish penicillin!), *crême caramel*, chopped herring and delicacies of every description. We often talked of how important these acts of generosity were to us. Through them Percy could feel that these people actually 'willed' him well.

Percy spent the first couple of weeks at home preparing for the Journal Club meeting as if his life depended upon it. It was the first real obstacle he had to overcome that was unrelated to his illness. Although he was an unassuming man, he prided himself on being able to lecture well. He always appeared to speak off the cuff, but this was an illusion, as he always prepared everything meticulously. This talk had to be better than any other, as he did not want his peers to think that his faculties were in any way impaired.

He looked ill on the day I drove him to the lecture hall, and his clothes just hung on him. He was pale and weak, and I longed for the talk to be over so that I could take him back home to rest on his bed. The couple of hours I spent waiting for the meeting to finish were interminable. I prayed that all would go well and that Percy would not break down while he was speaking. I need not have worried. Apparently the meeting went extremely well, and he presented the lecture, to a full house, in his usual good form.

Although the lecture imposed a tremendous strain on Percy, it proved to be a turning point in his progress. It was as if he had come to terms with his position and had decided to make the best of everything. He had always been a very gentle, caring person, but he seemed to develop an extra dimension of discernment, and for the first time in his life he was not afraid to show his feelings. David also was aware of this:

It was as if he had been given new sources of energy, as if he had been granted new insights into disease and the world in general. His patience and interest seemed infinite. These qualities were not new to him, but at this time they seemed enhanced.

Once Percy had regained his confidence, there was no stopping him. He cheerfully told David:

I'm going overseas. I mean not now, but soon, and I'm coming back to work next month [on the hospital staff]. And then Ethel and I are both going overseas again. And we might throw away a little money on a roulette table. And I must say that I am feeling very well indeed, really well. I want to drop in on some friends in London and visit some places I know. It's all organized!

He paused, telling him rather diffidently:

Dudley has decided to give me chemotherapy. Just a few injections every now and then, sort of adjuvant chemotherapy, in case anything might happen. And also a small field of irradiation, just in case . . . Well, who knows, it might do some good. I'm bald already! [This was a reference to the fact that chemotherapy has the unpleasant side-effect of making the patient's hair fall out.] I'll let you know how I get along. Thank you once again for looking after me.

Now, although this allusion to his baldness was lightly passed off in his conversation with David, the issue assumed enormous proportions for Percy. The few hairs he had at the back of his head were as important to him as if he had a glorious head of hair, and their loss affected his self-esteem. Walking into the lifts of our flat, surrounded by mirrors, he positively shuddered when he looked at himself, and as a result he perpetually kept his head covered. I teased him and said that I was convinced that he would rather be seen naked than bald.

Many patients who undergo chemotherapy worry about losing their hair more than about any other side-effect the treatment might have. I feel that something should be done to confront and allay this worry, perhaps even before the treatment begins. Because of Percy's distress I persuaded him to have a hairpiece made. It proved a terrible problem. It is one thing to wear a wig covering your whole head, but to try to get a hairpiece to stick around the perimeter of the head is another matter. The wig-maker was a man of infinite patience and great sympathy, and he spent many hours trying to satisfy us. The result was by no means perfect (most of us preferred Percy with no hair), but he said that he felt less naked in it. It took us over half an hour every morning to fix the thing in place with double-sided sticky tape, since we had to make sure that it was centrally positioned and secure. Fortunately, we had lots of laughs over the hairpiece, and it became another shared experience.

The first time Percy wore it was a memorable occasion. I had warned our two grandchildren of eight and four that Grandpa had lost his hair because of the treatment he was receiving, and I told them that temporarily he was going to have artificial hair. I asked them not to remark on it or to stare unduly. Obediently they walked in and kissed him as usual, without saying anything, and they looked not at him but past him. They sat on the couch opposite Percy, at the furthest point from him. They nearly twisted their heads off their bodies trying to see him without 'looking' at him. It was so funny that we all burst out laughing, and that broke the tension. We let them examine the source of amusement, and from then on it was easy going.

September–December 1980

Three months after his operation Percy decided to attend a meeting of a breast cancer group of which he had been an active member for years. It was to take place in Nice. David encouraged him to accept the invitation, and Dudley arranged his treatment accordingly.

Percy's decision to go to Nice on his own was very traumatic for me. I really did not want him to go, and certainly not on his own, but he persuaded me that it was important for him to undertake this trip alone. He felt that it would give him back his self-confidence, and the doctors all agreed. It was sheer willpower that got him through this ordeal. I doubt whether many other people would have succeeded as he did. He described his own feelings on tape:

> Immediately after my first treatment I actually went to Nice. I felt dreadful but I *schlepped* [dragged myself] there. I was disappointed at the hotel but was happy to be in the company of my colleagues and friends. [When we had viewed this hotel on a previous trip we thought that actually staying there must be the height of luxury.]
>
> I flew back to Johannesburg, where I attended a most interesting controversial discussion about surgical topics. I took part in this and presented two short papers in the discussion and sat on two panels. I met some very interesting people.
>
> I was wearing a hairpiece for the first time, and was extremely embarrassed, although everyone behaved most perfectly. I wasn't very good at fixing the hairpiece, and it slipped quite a number of times. This particularly happened one evening when I went to a restaurant. I ordered curried beef while I was with some people. Now, when I eat curry or *peri-peri*, I perspire. My face perspires; my forehead perspires; and my bald head perspires. It loosened all the tags of my wig, and I felt my wig *very slowly* slipping to the back of my head, and there was nothing I could do about it. I kept pulling it forward and touching it, and I didn't know whether the others noticed it, but I became acutely aware of my predicament. I decided there and then that I mustn't eat curry or *peri-peri* because of this problem of sweating. Actually, if I can get over the cytotoxic drugs and my hair grows again, I'd love to do away with the damn wig.

Although this trip was a tremendous strain on Percy physically, he returned with a very positive attitude towards living and working.

We both thought that a complete break from routine would be advisable after his second course of injections, but because of a drop in his blood count he was feeling very weak and lethargic, and our timing was wrong. We both realized that the time to go on holiday is when you are feeling well, to enable you to feel even stronger; you should not try to force recovery. Percy noted:

> When I felt a little better and the treatment was temporarily discontinued we went to Sun City [a casino in one of the African states] for a few days. I wasn't up to the enjoyment of the place, although it was magnificent. I played the tables but couldn't enjoy the food.

We had to pass through Johannesburg before reaching the casino, so we stopped off for a few days to see various members of the family. Because Percy was feeling so ill, he was convinced that it would be the last time he would see them all, and we arranged to meet them for tea at a favourite cousin's home. Everyone was upset to see Percy's changed appearance. The conversation was very stilted and the atmosphere strained. As soon as they all started reminiscing and joking about the past, however, he became his old self again. Even the tone of his voice became stronger. We had a lovely afternoon. Originally I thought that this get-together would be macabre, almost like a pre-funeral wake, but I did not raise any objections as I realized that Percy's wishes should be accorded priority. Again I was proved wrong in my assessment of the situation, and again Percy appreciated his own achievement.

On our arrival in Sun City all he wanted to do was have a hot bath and crawl into bed. No sooner had he submerged himself in the water than there was a frantic phone call from the hotel manager to ask him to attend to one of the guests, who had collapsed. When he heard me trying to make excuses, he grabbed the phone, inquired where the patient was and, after hurriedly getting dressed, careered down the corridor to the other end of the hotel like a young athlete. Percy's transformation from patient to doctor was remarkable. I was suddenly acutely aware of how important it was for him to be allowed to contribute his skill and knowledge as long as he was alive. He diagnosed a coronary thrombosis and took complete charge of the patient's welfare; it may have been one of those rare occasions when a doctor actually saves a patient's life.

When we returned to our flat we were much more relaxed about living with our problems. We knew that there would be difficulties along the path, but it was as if the acute phase of the illness were over and we felt fully prepared to accept the future.

Many young doctors who have completed their training in their own home towns arrange to travel overseas in order to further their studies, as Percy himself did. This was what Gillian and Jeff had been planning, and Percy was adamant that his illness should in no way affect their plans. Both Gillian and Percy were in an ambivalent position; they did not want to be parted from each other, yet both were aware that they had to face every eventuality. Gillian had expressed her feelings at the time of Percy's operation:

> I wished secretly that he wouldn't survive the postoperative period. I wanted him to die suddenly and without having to go through all the difficulties that he would otherwise have to face. We were planning to travel overseas searching for jobs, but I didn't feel good about leaving my family.

This was probably a normal reaction, but a quick and painless death would have deprived Percy of what he described as the best time of his life. So many of us think that we know what we want and how we would behave in certain circumstances, but we never discover what our desires really are or how we will respond to events until the circumstances arise.

The parting at the airport was devastating for us all, but once Gillian and Jeff had left our fears turned out to be unfounded. Percy recorded these words:

> Their parting was a traumatic experience for me because I felt sure that I would never see them again. We phoned them quite often and heard about their wonderful trip. This eased the mental trauma of their departing tremendously.

And we had many wonderfully happy times together after this and even visited them in Canada, where they both decided to specialize.

There is much controversy over various treatments with drugs for patients with cancer, particularly forms of cancer for which some doctors might believe that cytotoxic treatment has no real value. Before Percy developed cancer of the colon he was not convinced that postoperative treatment was an advantage, yet when he was advised to have this treatment he reluctantly agreed. The strange thing was that Percy was deeply distressed, once the treatment had commenced, if for any reason it had to be delayed. Every patient reacts differently to these drugs, and even the same patient reacts differently to the same drugs at various stages. There is no denying that some (but not all) patients feel very ill indeed as a result of the treatment and may want to discontinue, but in most cases this is only a transient reaction. This was the case with Percy at only one stage of his treatment:

The cytotoxic therapy has really been a problem to me. I have recently had another five-day course of injections, and I know it was meant for my good, but it caused a tremendous reaction and complications as far as I am concerned, although most of the oncologists thought it was just minor. Firstly, I felt terrible, and I felt weak. I bled from my nose and I bled from my rectum. I developed purpuric spots [little red spots on the skin]. My appetite was completely gone, and for about ten days life was just not worth living. I have come to the conclusion that I am never going to have that dose again. I'll either have a much smaller dose, which I have had before, which didn't affect me so badly, or none, no matter what the consequences.

I've never realized how important quality of life is. Quality of life is much more important than quantity of life. I never thought about it like this when I taught students, when I worked with breast cancer. I would map out a five-year survival plan and not really think of the quality of those five years. Now I know that it is much better to live one year, two years, with a better quality of life than five years just surviving. So I'm not going to have that sort of reaction again.

This was probably the worst time, as Percy was at his lowest ebb; nevertheless, he continued to concern himself with other people's problems. He started organizing a visit of the British Association of Surgical Oncologists, joined in the discussions and even read a couple of papers. David was aware of his condition and wrote:

His life was most certainly not morbidly involved with the disease, but in his mind was the Damocletian sword, and his body suffered the side-effects of the therapy. He hid this successfully and completely from his colleagues. In fact, it was a serene and optimistic Percy on ward rounds, a warm, wise and wittily anecdotal surgeon talking to registrars and housemen. It was at this time that he presented a *tour de force* on breast cancer at the hospital: a packed lecture theatre, two simultaneous projectors and the authority talking on his subject. He had two complex articles accepted for publication. He steered and guided the international breast trial.

The Association presented Percy with a shield for the valuable work he had done, and this was a wonderful boost to his morale, as he acknowledged on tape:

I was overwhelmed by the visit of the British Association of Surgical Oncologists, whose visit I initially started planning . . . I was completely overwhelmed by them presenting me with a shield for the work I had been doing. I was overwhelmed by the fact that David McKenzie [the dean] had singled me out as someone who had done some work. I read a paper that day and even chaired a meeting. How I did it I don't know, but I was happy that I was able to do it. So, no matter what happens to me, I want quality of life and not quantity.

To Percy, work and achievement meant quality of life.

He managed to keep going until after this meeting, even though he was feeling very ill. Because of his very low state of health and a drop in his white blood cell count he was especially prone to infection, which can cause serious complications. Unfortunately, Percy developed an ear infection, which in itself was not serious but a high temperature brought resulting rigors.

A rigor can be a very frightening experience for anyone who has not witnessed it before, and it can occur without warning. In the case of a mild rigor the patient feels cold and shivers slightly; if the rigor is severe, the patient shakes and shudders so violently that you think he may fall out of bed. The most important thing is to keep calm, to apply hot-water bottles and light blankets until the shivering has ceased and then to wash the patient with a cool sponge, concentrating particularly on the face, the neck and the extremities, to reduce the fever.

Although the doctors would have preferred Percy to remain at home to prevent any further cross-infection at this stage, they were forced to admit him to hospital in order to administer intravenous antibiotics. Once again, his knowledge of this serious complication may have caused him to over-react, but I believe that for him this was the worst period of his illness. He had to be nursed in isolation. Anyone who entered his room had to be dressed in a long white gown, a cap and a mask. No visitors were permitted. Being alone in the room all day, with me like a ghost in white, must only have added to his extreme depression. Each day seemed like a year, particularly as his temperature did not drop and his white blood cell count did not rise (in fact, it reached an alarmingly low level). I was so desperate at this stage that I begged the doctors to lie and tell him that there was some improvement, but this they refused to do.

While he was lying in bed for those six days, his thoughts were only about death and dying; he was convinced that he would succumb to his disease, as he repeatedly told me. Later, however, he recorded these thoughts:

In all this time Ethel has been – I cannot tell you – too fantastic. She washed me, fed me, clothed me and looked after me. She has never murmured or complained about anything. She's only been interested in my welfare: how I was feeling, whether I would eat, whether my weight was going up. She insisted on my not getting too hot or too cold, on sleeping, on resting and trying to get me stronger by walking. If I didn't want to go out, she never mentioned that she wanted to go. I knew that she wanted to go, but if I didn't want to go anywhere, she was quite happy just staying at home. Then she was always so optimistic and so helpful. She never wore a long face. She always said it will be better, that I would be better, that I would be all right. Fortunately, she had quite a few things to attend to – she always had things to do. She had to decide about our house, in which we were not living – whether we should do alterations to make it into two town houses (which was very feasible), whether we should sell the house or re-let it again. These became her problems, and I took no particular part in the decisions except in giving the odd advice, which I was not really fit to give. You see, when you become depressed, as I have become, you don't want to get involved. You just don't want to concern yourself in other things (I didn't even want to read anything, even the newspapers) or concern yourself with other people's problems, even though you must try and be the same person.

I even played bowls again – the members of the Glen Club made me so welcome.

The sustenance and help of our friends has been so marvellous . . .

Then there is Lawrence, who has to live under the cloud of a sick father. He has to restrict himself, perhaps too young to understand the significance of all these problems. I think of my whole family, who have only given me joy. I've never had any serious problems. I know that my family are reasonably well provided for, and I have no real fear. My grandchildren, Dennis's and Michele's children, Adie and Larry, are absolute bundles of joy. I see a great future for all my children, wherever they may go, and this pleases me. I feel that perhaps Ethel and I had a lot to do with it, and it gives me a sense of tremendous achievement.

At this moment I remember . . . so many people who meant so much to me . . . Above all else I think of Ethel, the only person that meant everything to me and whom I have loved more than words can tell.

I am not afraid of death. I've come to terms with myself, and I know that all people die, some sooner and some later. What I do fear is dying, the actual act of dying. I don't want to have prolonged suffering if it can possibly be helped. I can quote from a poem by the late Samuel B. Chyatte:*

> I am a victim, I am a victor,
> For death will win its waiting game.
> Momentarily I have tricked her,
> Fanned life's fading flame.
> But life is worth living, uncertain day to day
> When you can be doing – giving –
> When the world heeds what you say.
> Leave me without purpose, and take my self-esteem,
> As well as leave me lifeless,
> And only alive on a machine.

Enough of my emotion – I wish to be cremated, and prayers for one night only. Good-bye.

Once Percy had overcome the setback relating to the chemotherapy he no longer thought about dying. When his condition improved the doctors were able to give him blood transfusions, after which he made a rapid recovery. Dudley discussed the setback and subsequent investigations:

Whilst holidaying in England after attending meetings in America I was upset to receive a telephone call from South Africa telling me that Percy had been admitted to hospital in rather a poor state. He had had an adverse reaction to the drug therapy which I had prescribed prior to my departure . . .

Immediately on my return to South Africa I went to see Percy. The period in hospital had been rather disturbing to him. He had obviously been very ill, and the episode had jolted him physically as well as emotionally. We discussed further management, and I could see that he was now very fearful of receiving further

---

*Extensive research has failed to find the origin of this poem, though Samuel Chyatte was a doctor who was maintained on dialysis for two years.

chemotherapy. He did not want, under any circumstances, to have a repeat of his recent experience. I agreed with him, and it was decided that we should perhaps investigate him to see whether his disease process was stable, regressing or progressing, before prescribing any more drug therapy. After much joint discussion, it was decided that a body scan [CAT scan] should be performed to determine the effect of the therapy.

We both entered into this investigation with a lot of fear, Percy being worried about the procedure and what the outcome would be. My main fear was what I was to tell him if the disease process had progressed. Thankfully, the scan was totally successful. There was no evidence of residual disease, and there was evidence that the disease had not spread to the liver. This was indeed cause for celebration. We had been able to share our fears together, which had been a valuable experience.

Today, a body scan (CAT scan) is almost a routine method of investigation, but Percy described it as a painful mental experience. Because of his vast knowledge of what they could find, he was in two minds about consenting to having it done. Dudley must have realized his quandary and very thoughtfully arranged for the scan to be done without delay.

In the hospital the area where the scanning machines were placed was not within easy reach of suitable waiting-rooms, and Percy had to wait in a draughty corridor. He was dressed in a cotton gown, which made him feel that he had lost his dignity as well as his identity. The radiologist, radiographers and nursing staff were magnificent in the execution of their duties, but I could not help wondering if they were always aware of how bewildered and frightened a patient might be. There is perhaps a danger that the greater the technical skills and equipment available to us, the less we treat the patient as a person. I did not know who needed more sympathy – Percy, who knew too much, or many of the other patients, who had no idea what was going on. I felt strongly, as I waited for Percy, that there should be a body of caring people whose job is to be with the patients at such times, to explain what is happening and to hold their hands and listen to their fears.

Percy described his feelings during this procedure as those of a man on trial: he sensed that he was fighting for his very life. In the end he could hardly believe the verdict: all was well. He and I both cried with relief, and Dudley and David were present to celebrate and share our joy.

January–December 1981

The next year, 1981, started off as a very good one. Percy was back at work full-time, and he led a normal life, at times even forgetting that he had been ill. He went to London to another breast cancer conference and met a number of old friends, who were delighted with his progress and general condition.

He was always a keen observer of the political scene and was upset at missing the election in South Africa. This did not prevent him from writing a letter, published in a local paper, headed 'Did They Die in Vain?':

> I am dismayed to learn of Jewish Nationalist candidates, supporters and workers in the forthcoming election. I can understand Afrikaner feeling and know their historical struggle for freedom and dignity, for a place in the sun. I cannot understand support by Jews for a party that has enshrined naked discrimination in law. How can people with a proud tradition going back four thousand years support laws that destroy family life, forcibly remove thousands of people from their homes and businesses simply to satisfy the greed of white nationalism? How can you support discrimination in salaries [doctors' and nurses'] simply on basis of skin colour, forbid love across the colour line, and punish an innocent woman who strolls across a 'white beach'?
>
> Not more than four decades ago our brothers and sisters died in gas chambers. Their crime? They were Jews, the victims of discrimination. I lie awake at night trembling at the thought (may God forgive us). Did they die in vain?

This was the old Percy, involved with any cause against discrimination of any sort.

Gillian and Jeff returned from their overseas trip and told us that they had decided to take up appointments in Toronto, where they would both further their medical studies. But they rented a furnished flat near us while working for a further three months, and we all felt that this was a terrific bonus, as we saw them daily.

We decided to travel to the Transvaal with them for a week before they were due to leave, and we had one of the most wonderful holidays of our lives. Percy had put on weight, and he felt and looked well. We played bowls, went to shows, walked, ate, drank, talked incessantly and laughed a lot.

Of course, it was sad seeing the children off at the airport a second time. Gillian clung to Percy, wondering how long this remission could last, but the moment of goodbye was not nearly as bad as when they had first left, soon after the operation.

Back in Cape Town Percy got straight into the swing of work and continued feeling well. One day he told me that he had agreed to give a talk about cancer based on his experience of thirty years. I had been proud of him on many occasions, but my pride at that moment surpassed anything I had felt before. He decided to call the lecture 'Thoughts in the Mind of a Patient Living with Cancer', and he delivered it to a large audience that had gathered to commemorate the fiftieth anniversary of the South African National Cancer Association. I later found the notes that Percy had made while preparing it, and the following points are those which he had underlined for particular emphasis:

How do you live with a thought that you have a very limited time left? Do you splurge and run overseas and spend money? Do you stop working? Do you just lie about waiting for the end to come?

I decided to work even harder and live as if I have a normal life ahead of me and to achieve as much as possible.

My big problem is to plan for the future where there is no future. I would like to tell my story but feel that it has all been said before.

How do I start? I think as a doctor with patients, you must start with humility.

From these first thoughts the lecture developed into a lucid summary of the experience of cancer patients, deftly balanced between professional concern and personal reflection.

Thoughts in the Mind of a Patient Living with Cancer

Over the last twenty-five years I have dealt with large numbers of patients suffering from malignant disease. Mercifully, many patients have been cured, but the majority have had to contend with persistent, recurrent or overwhelming disease. I never ceased to admire the courage and fortitude of these patients. Their obedience, trust and hope have only emphasized the limits of our ability and sadness of our experience. Like Professor Milton who has described the problem so beautifully, I feel that the thoughts of patients with cancer pass through different stages and often overlap or may be arrested in those who are unable to adjust to the realization of the progress of the disease. It is not only the thoughts of patients which have interested me – I have tried to fathom our medical attitude to the desperate problems of these patients, and I cannot but have a sneaking regard for Anton Chekhov, who said, 'I have made a point all my life of mistrusting all doctors, lawyers and women – they are shammers and deceivers.'

The initial shock can be so severe that although you hear the words, they do not really penetrate the consciousness. There may be patients who do not want to accept the truth, but I believe that every effort should be made to discuss the situation. The timing of this discussion is most important, and the doctor should never evade the issue. There should be an unhurried consultation, preferably in the company of the wife or husband or someone close, and try to let the patient feel that he is never alone in his predicament. When you are told you have cancer, it is like a nightmare or as if there is an explosion in your head.

The doctor should be honest at all times with the patient and encourage him to talk about his fears and worries, however trivial they may seem. There must be a basic confidence between the doctor and patient, and stress must be made on the unpredictability of cancer. Even when problems arise, there should always be a sense of hope. Where all treatment is concerned the doctor should show concern and compassion, and humility is always a good starting point. I believe that the doctor should stress the favourable points about the illness or operation and point out why there should be a good prognosis, particularly when the whole tumour has been removed. When I was young I was unable to relate to the patient. Nowadays I do tell the truth, and I have always been satisfied with this position because I could develop a true patient–doctor relationship, and there was always mutual trust throughout the patient's illness.

There are the accepted reactions to knowing that you are seriously ill: shock, denial, fear, anger, anxiety, depression and, hopefully, acceptance.

Let me describe the four stages I have experienced with my patients as well as myself. Some stages overlap, and some are arrested.

How does one adjust to the realization and progress of the disease?

Stage 1

When the patient realizes that the illness could be malignant. The condition often presents with trivial signs – no pain, no loss of strength. There may be a period of serious symptoms, and he suspects he has cancer. He feels the icy fingers of impending death.

The patient is afraid – the fear of the unknown, the fear of leaving loved ones behind, the fear of pain, the fear of the operation and the very real fear of dying. He is even afraid of revealing himself as a coward. I remember fearing that I would be the object of pity.

Stage 2

When cancer has been established, usually after the operation – and the operation may have been very successful, with possible cure of cancer. The patient often suspects that the truth or whole truth has not been told him by his doctor or his family. He analyses everything and every facial expression of the surgeon, the registrar, the intern, the nursing sister, the nurse and even the porter. He listens to every word that is being said or for those not being said. Often the patient does not want to hear the truth, and the facts may have to be repeated to him and his family over and over.

An emotion which is very common is – why me? Why should

this happen? I never did anybody any harm. I never had any luck. There is often self-pity and resentment and a feeling that no one understands you and does not care. The worst of all emotions is that of absolute loneliness which engulfs you. There is depression and irritability, which might change your whole personality and make you unpleasant with a deep dislike of some people. Many develop a kind of isolation from the community. Solzhenitsyn, in his book *Cancer Ward*, describes the tumour like a wall behind the patient, the patient on one side and the family and loved ones on the other. Loneliness becomes overwhelming in the dark hours of the night, and it is essential to prescribe correctly for these symptoms.

The greatest comfort of all is having an understanding family. This was the time beyond all others that I realized how much I loved my wife and how much I needed her. She had an iron steadfastness and courage, and there was a fathomless emotion which enabled us to face things together. To the world it was a stiff upper lip, but between us there were no secrets. We both realized at the beginning that talking about things together is so much easier than thinking about them on your own.

After surgery I can describe my own experience. I felt that I was delving into the bowels of the earth. I had x-ray therapy and I had a personal vendetta with those machines looming over me. Would they fall on me? I felt so alone with the machine positively spluttering at me.

After this initial reaction you begin to feel that this machine is vital in the process of curing you, and the smiling young radiographers, who are so kind, give you courage and hope.

The cytotoxic drugs are the worst, as they make you feel so ill and depressed. Yet, funnily enough, when for some reason or other you are unable to proceed with the treatment, you *will* your blood count to improve so that you are able to continue with these very drugs that you have previously dreaded.

The problem with cancer treatment, whether you are well or not, is that you have to return for follow-up check-ups regularly, and you are never completely free of medical or hospital attention. It interferes with living – but even this you learn to accept.

One of the most important facts about convalescing is to stay at home until you are really well enough to do most things. Never go on holiday with the hope of speeding up your recovery. You will only feel angry and frustrated if you are unable to enjoy the amenities available. Wait to get well, and then you will enjoy everything so much more.

There comes a time when the disease might recur and the patient can only have palliative therapy. The reactions of the patient vary from high spirits to utter despair, and this is the time when the family and medical support is so important. Not only is there the very real fear of death but also the fear of losing dignity, which to me is the greatest fear of all. Most of us are unfamiliar with death and think of it as belonging to the senile or elderly. How do we really react to death ourselves?

(1) Acceptance, which is very rare. Here people with deep religious beliefs find it much easier to cope.

(2) Withdrawal, which is much commoner and much more difficult to handle. There is terrible depression, and there is tension in the whole family, as everyone is afraid to say or do the wrong thing.

(3) Denial. The patient just cannot believe that this is happening to him. He might listen to what the doctor says but know that the doctor is wrong. These patients may exhibit a remarkable bon-homie and arrive at outpatients laughing and joking and interfering with the other patients. These patients are sitting targets for quacks. These people are really so afraid and desperate and are usually unable to communicate and share their fears. These are the people who spend so much money on unnecessary treatment, which at best is useless and could be very harmful as well.

(4) This stage might arise when the patient is dying. These patients are happiest at home, if this is possible. They are familiar with their surroundings and loved ones. Obviously we do not necessarily have the choice, and you must be guided by the experience of your doctor. If the patient is in hospital, it is imperative never to let him feel alone and unwanted. When very little can actively be done for the patient the doctor so often ignores the dying patient, and he seems to feel, 'What – that patient still in my ward?' What he really feels is embarrassment at his failure to help the patient, and yet he can really do so much. The correct medication for the arising symptoms – depression, pain, sleeplessness – and, more important than all, the human element of knowing that one is loved and cared for.

The attitude and behaviour of doctors is so important. As I originally stated and repeat, communication between the patient, his doctor and the family is vital. When a patient realizes that he has been told a pack of lies, he regards his surgeon or doctor with suspicion, fearing that he is incompetent and dishonest. It is all too easy for the surgeon to close the abdomen that has evidence of cancer and metastases, slap the patient on the back and congratulate him on coming through the operation so well. He then sends the patient back to the general practitioner with a note saying that the patient will be dead within six months. This surgeon may be fine technically and his treatment may be very good for his own bank account, but what a very poor doctor!

To say to the patient who is incurable, 'I do not need to see you again' is like throwing both ends of a rope to a drowning person. One should always be aware of the unpredictibility of cancer, when patients can live well for many years, even with metastases, and often might die from an entirely different cause. So many of these patients outlive their doctors and are able to lead a full and productive life.

A doctor should never venture an exact prognosis – he will probably be wrong. Take care of what you predict. When some executives ask whether they should draw up their will and get their affairs in order, I always tell them to do so. Patients are often not as afraid of death as of being abandoned by their doctor and family in the face of death. Death is as natural as childbirth. Death holds no fearful threat. Living without life is hell. Death is natural. It may be just; it is often merciful; it ought always to be dignified. And who knows – it may be paradise. I wish to quote from Hans Züssner, the discoverer of poliomyelitis and himself a victim of cancer:

> How good that ere the winter comes I die,
> That ageless in your heart I'll come to rest,
> Serene and proud as when you loved me best.

Many of Percy's patients – some who had been cured of cancer and some who were living with the disease – attended the meeting. They came up to him afterwards and thanked him for putting their feelings into words. They said they felt better now that they knew others had experienced similar reactions. Percy thought that this alone made the effort worth while. I was so proud of him as he stood at the lectern, speaking with confidence, compassion and understanding, and he looked so well that the tears streamed unashamedly down my cheeks. Someone took a photograph of him as he spoke, and this is the way I will always remember him – humble, dignified and eager to help others.

Dudley was among the audience. Later he was to say:

> The paper was superbly presented with a great emotional over-tone. It was exceptionally well received by the audience, and it was extremely heartening to note that both his wife and daughter were in the audience to share in the audience response. I think that this was a very important milestone in their family circle, as it was a further demonstration of the deep relationship which existed between them all and which was to manifest itself through-out his illness.

Long periods followed when things went very well indeed, and we enjoyed life very much. Although there were family problems from time to time, we did not let them interfere with our awareness of how precious every day was to us.

There were times when Percy worried unduly about odd symptoms that he thought were sinister but proved to be nothing untoward. He developed a small lump behind the nipple of his breast, which David assured him was no more than mastitis (inflamation of the breast tissue). Then he developed rectal bleeding again, and it was decided to do another CAT scan. This time the procedure was not quite so frightening, but while we realized that one can adjust to anything, we were still very worried about the results.

Once again a reprieve – and how happy we all were. At this stage John, the professor of surgery, offered Percy a tremendous challenge in requesting him to sort out some difficulties at the Somerset, a teaching hospital. I still do not know whether he really required Percy for the job, but it did a great deal for his morale at a time when he badly needed a boost. Percy admitted to me that he did not know whether he would be able to fulfil his obligations satisfactorily, but I reassured him by saying that John would never have asked him if he had any doubts in his mind.

Percy loved working at the Somerset Hospital, although he was feeling tired and ill as a result of the treatment he was receiving. The excitement with which he went to work every day was a wonderful stimulant for him. Whether the people with whom he worked were aware of how ill he was or whether Percy managed to bring out the best in his colleagues, the fact remains that he sorted out the problems, and a new team spirit grew among the doctors and the nursing staff.

As Percy mentioned on one of his tapes, when a person becomes very seriously ill he often closes his mind to other people's problems. It came as a shock to him to notice suddenly how ill his brother Morris appeared. Then Morris was admitted to Groote Schuur Hospital for investigations. It was discovered that he had developed a serious type of leukaemia. Percy was extremely worried about his condition and even remarked that Morris would probably die before he did. His words proved prophetic: Morris died a couple of days after admission.

It was a blessing at this sad time that Percy had the challenge of the new post at the Somerset to think about. He was terribly distressed by the death of his brother and repeatedly asked, 'How is it possible that Morris has died? I am the sick one.'

Another considerate suggestion that John made was that Percy and I should combine a visit to the children, Gillian and Jeff, in Canada with attendance at a breast cancer meeting in Berne. This meant an extra couple of weeks' leave soon after putting the new programme into action at the Somerset. Normally Percy would not have considered leaving a new post at such a time, but because things were running so smoothly – or perhaps because he had a premonition about his future – he was very anxious to arrange this trip.

Dudley commented:

I was very happy with Percy's plan to consult a friend of his who was a senior surgeon in London. I was also happy with the idea of his holidaying overseas and delighted that he would be able to see his daughter and son-in-law, who were both medically trained and who were newly settled in the new home and country. I was heartened by the fact that Percy was going to see somebody of international status about his condition.

Dudley organized a further course of cytotoxic drugs before our departure. Percy felt ill as a result, and apart from going to work daily he took things very easily, with plenty of rest. Meals were a problem, as he had no appetite, and I had to tempt him with small, appetizing meals. There are many fortified foods on the market, but I found that when Percy was already nauseous, these often made him feel even more ill. However little he enjoyed, it was preferable to forcing down proteins, vitamins and calories. Percy did not lose weight, however, which was good for his morale. My yardstick was whether there was a movement after meals to the cupboard where the chocolates were kept, and as long as I heard the click of the cupboard door I was happy.

We decided that I would leave for Toronto a few days before Percy, as he was going first to the meeting in Berne, and I preferred to spend this time in Canada. Although I had travelled overseas on business on previous occasions, it was never without Percy, who did all the organizing. I resented all his detailed instructions and laughingly told him that he treated me like an imbecile. He had good reason to doubt my capabilities. When I reached London en route to Vancouver I lost my keys as well as my purse containing my credit card. Fortunately, this was found by the cabin steward on the plane. This mishap was followed by the loss of all my luggage when I arrived in Vancouver. This was really not my fault, but I had trouble convincing Percy of my innocence when we met up in Toronto.

I had a wonderful time in Vancouver visiting friends whom we had met while Percy was studying in London, and I had a few days with Gill and Jeff in Toronto before Percy arrived. I was pleased to see how well they had adjusted to their new life. We ran from morning to night, trying to fit twenty-four hours into twelve, and I confess that it was good to have someone else to assume all responsibilities for a change and not to have to think for myself.

We met Percy at the airport and were relieved to see how well he was looking. He had had a very successful meeting in Berne, where everyone had made a great fuss of him; academically too it had been very stimulating. The co-ordinator of the Ludwig Breast Cancer Group wrote of him after this meeting:

> The quality of the collaboration which we experienced with him was superb, but he was even more impressive for his primary concern, obvious in all the discussions in which he took part within the Group, for the patient herself, her suffering and destiny. We are grateful to Percy for his constant reminder.

Percy was excited to see the children in their new home, and they delighted him by doing everything possible to make him feel welcome.

We did notice that he had an irritating cough, which he said he had picked up before leaving South Africa. It caused Jeff concern, but he did not make an issue of it. On the second day Percy was very tired, and although we attempted some sightseeing, we could see that he was not up to it. We were fortunately able to discuss everything very freely, and at the outset we made some sensible plans. We decided that Percy should set the pace and do only what he felt up to, without any unnecessary strain. When we were at home he lay on a sofa like a lord. He watched television, which fascinated him, and he loved meeting all the children's friends and hearing of their work and experiences in Canada. We again made the mistake of leaving home when Percy was not feeling well, but Percy insisted on carrying out our plan to go by car to Montreal and Quebec.

We had our first taste of real winter weather. Snow covered the ground, the trees and the buildings and gave everything in sight a fairyland quality. We stayed in a beautiful old hotel in

Montreal and enjoyed a delicious meal in the French Quarter. It was freezing cold, well below zero. With the prospect of the temperatures dropping still further, Gillian felt very anxious about her father and insisted that we return to the warmth and comfort of their flat immediately.

Morris's son, who is a general practitioner in Toronto, was very concerned about Percy's condition and tried to persuade him to go into hospital for investigations. This Percy flatly refused to do, as he was well aware that this was no ordinary chest complaint that he had but complications resulting from the cancer. Despite the fact that he was ill, he was happy and relaxed with the children and grateful that he had been able to make the journey.

There were times, as Percy lay asleep late at night, when we wondered whether he would deteriorate to such an extent that he would not make the flight back home. But he rallied and insisted that we should go back home via London, as arranged.

During Percy's illness we had reached a very good understanding of each other's problems, but there were times when the tension became too much for both of us, and there were explosions. The worst one was on our plane trip to London. On arriving at the airport I tried to change our tickets to first class for Percy's comfort. This was not possible, as the plane was full, but I managed to exchange his aisle seat for two seats in the middle bloc. He was so furious with me for interfering with the arrangements that we did not speak to each other for most of the journey. I was plunged into gloom and would not have minded if the plane had crashed.

When we arrived in London it was as if a magic wand had been waved over Percy. He blossomed and showed all his usual enthusiasm for the city.

Our friends Vera and Izzie, who now lived in London, spent many hours with us. We even had breakfast together. We had always been so compatible – no words were necessary between us – that we knew how solicitous they were of Percy's welfare. We spent four glorious days and evenings together, walking the streets of London, eating at restaurants and seeing quite a number of shows. Although Percy rested for a couple of hours each afternoon, it was hard to believe that he was really very ill.

Our big vice had always been the casinos, and we were members of a gambling club attached to one of the large hotels. We were too ashamed to tell our friends where we were going when they bade us goodnight, clearly thinking that we were having early nights; as soon as they departed we hopped into the nearest taxi and played the tables until the early hours of the morning. We giggled like a couple of children at our deception, and when I watched Percy's animated face while he was placing his chips on the table, I was thrilled that he was enjoying life so much.

The flight back to Cape Town was a complete contrast to the one to London – we laughed, reminisced, played Scrabble and were both very content.

As soon as we arrived at the flat I phoned Dudley to tell him how ill Percy had been. It was only then that I learned that Percy had not been well when he left Cape Town but had not mentioned this to anyone in case he was prevented from leaving. Dudley takes up the story:

I was phoned on the Sunday morning on which Percy and Ethel returned from their trip to hear that Percy had been desperately sick. The story soon emerged. In point of fact, Ethel had left ahead of Percy, and while she was overseas he had contracted a respiratory-tract infection in Cape Town. He had not placed himself on antibiotics and had actually forced himself on to the plane to Switzerland with a raging fever. The trip had been a success in that he had delivered his paper, had seen friends and had been encouraged by their reports about his health, but he was not well enough to enjoy the holiday part of the visit.

On his return he was once again investigated, and to our horror it was apparent that the disease had now gone beyond the realms of therapy. The next three months were painful not only to the patient and his loved ones but also certainly to the medical colleagues who knew him and would continue to care for him. It was during this phase that I visited him very frequently at his home and discussed with him the outcome of his condition. He was at all times fully aware of the future and had made all plans that were necessary. He had even gone as far as making tape recordings of his feelings about his final illness.

The one thing we discussed in depth was whether the patient should be told the full extent of his condition. Percy had always been a very busy surgeon, which necessitated handling patients with malignancy. He admitted that if he could have his time again, he would certainly be more open with his patients, would discuss their diagnoses in greater depth. This revealed the typical surgeon's approach to malignancy in that the patient is not made entirely aware of his condition or what the future holds for him.

Percy's own account revealed his feelings:

I knew that I was sick in November; in fact I had a lot of chest complaints. In spite of feeling sick I had to go overseas to attend a breast cancer conference particularly dealing with our breast clinic. I wanted to help in starting a new trial, and I was able to organize a new protocol for the Berne Breast Clinic in November 1981.

Another great step was that I was able to see my daughter and son-in-law in Toronto, which was something I was so looking forward to doing. In fact, I did more things in 1981 than I had done in my whole life.

I think that my experience of this whole illness taught me many things. Firstly, my reappraisal of my situation, a limited appraisal. I knew that there was nothing long-term about me any more. I also knew that planning was impossible, but quite remarkably I was able to do some of the things which I had originally thought were impossible. I was able to travel and to do so many things. Recovering from the operation and being aware of the severity of the problem, I was surprised at how much I could still do. I would like to point out to people who have similar problems that they should really make use of every minute of every day while they are still able to do so and to achieve things. Do not throw in the towel but carry on. Sometimes you can be well for a long time, and this precious time must not be wasted.

All these achievements pleased me immensely and gave me so much comfort that I felt I had achieved more than was possible

under the circumstances. In fact, I felt I had been given borrowed
time just to do all these things.

Interestingly, this tape was made twelve months after the one
quoted on pages 58–60 and indicates how, in that time, Percy
had adjusted to the circumstances.

December was a bad month for Percy, as he had an extremely
high sedimentation rate, which indicated underlying problems.
He still went to work at the Somerset Hospital daily but was
physically exhausted. Although we did not go out socially, we
had many visitors, and Percy was content.

The 16th of December is a public holiday in South Africa. We
were entertaining friends and family to tea when the telephone
rang. It was my nephew to tell me that my brother Norman had
just dropped dead. How was it possible that Norman, who had
been such a support to both of us, could possibly be dead?
Although he had had problems over the previous couple of
years, I never realized that he had a serious heart condition. I
suppose I was so involved with Percy that I excluded everyone
else from my mind.

We were shocked and quiet in the car as we rushed to be with
my sister-in-law. Our thoughts were in a turmoil. Percy was very
ill, and with no warning Norman had died – and so soon after
Morris. I was distraught, but at this stage I was even more
concerned about how the news would affect Percy. I could not
allow myself the privilege of despair, and I think that this is the
reason for my extreme sadness every time I think of Norman and
Morris.

The last weeks of the year passed very quietly. Percy and I
spent many hours in complete harmony. He had always been
reserved and undemonstrative in the past, but now he was warm
and affectionate, and we were completely at peace. We enjoyed
the flat; we loved watching the beautiful sunsets; and we
were delighted to welcome many overseas visitors, with whom
Percy reminisced.

At this time Lawrence and his friends were planning a trip
overseas. Percy's greatest worry was that nothing should interfere

with their arrangements. We organized a series of slide shows on London and the Continent, and Percy was quite boyish in his pleasure at talking of the places which we ourselves had enjoyed. There was fun and laughter and plenty of advice as we listened to their plans.

January–23 March 1982

January the 1st was Percy's birthday, and all day a continual stream of visitors arrived with gifts and good wishes. The nuns from the local nursing home, who were our great friends, came as they always did on this day, and Percy entertained us all by reminiscing about events of the past thirty years. It was balm for him to go over the highlights of his life and professional career.

Although Percy dreaded the prospect of distressing complications, when they actually happened he was quite resigned, and he accepted them with great dignity and fortitude. This time the x-rays showed that he had tumour deposits (secondaries) in the liver, ascites (fluid in the abdomen) and pleural effusion (fluid around the lungs). He taped a brief comment on his condition:

> In January 1982 I became very ill again and had to return to hospital, as it looked as if I'd developed an intestinal obstruction with ascites. I underwent a second operation when the ascites was tapped.

I was aware of the fact that Percy's abdomen was becoming distended and was developing an obstruction. I was aware too of how serious such a condition could be, and I think that was the first time I was prepared to accept the fact that he would never recover. We both knew when he was readmitted to hospital that probably nothing more could be done for him except to tap the fluid. We had tears in our eyes, but behind the tears we felt gratified that a wonderful love and understanding had developed between us.

This time Percy was admitted to the radiotherapy block, although he took no notice of where he was, as he was too ill to be interested in what was happening. Besides David, who was our pillar of strength, a visiting colleague from Baltimore was waiting for Percy to reassure him when he arrived. I spoke to him outside the ward. He was so distressed that I felt that it was he who needed the reassurance.

David decided to operate to relieve the obstruction as soon as possible, and Dudley was also present. One of the head matrons, a friend of Percy's, accompanied him to the operating theatre. They all departed together and left me waiting in the ward. I was so overcome by everyone's kindness that I broke down completely and cried, unaware of the passage of time. Suddenly there was a commotion outside the door: there was Percy being wheeled back into the ward with the whole entourage. Apparently there had been a mix-up over Percy's pathological reports, and they could not operate until they had sorted it out. It was like a scene in a farce. At any other time Percy and I would have laughed together, but on this occasion no one laughed. Fortunately, there was not much delay before the problems were solved, and by this time Michele had arrived. She accompanied Percy as well, which made him happy.

All I needed to do was to look at David's face to know the outcome of the operation. He had not given me any false hopes before the procedure, but he was clearly upset that his worst suspicions had been confirmed. He knew that both Gillian and Lawrence were overseas, and he promised me that he would advise me when he thought they should be sent for.

I asked him the imponderable question: how long did he think Percy could survive? He would not commit himself to a time limit.

During the first couple of days after the operation Percy's condition was critical, and I stayed with him day and night. The nurses and sisters were superb, and they even made a bed up in the ward, next to Percy's, to enable me to rest. The dreaded hiccoughs started again, which added to Percy's extreme distress.

Gillian phoned. On hearing the news, she decided to come back to South Africa on the first available plane. Lawrence contacted me from Munich, and though I tried to dissuade him from returning immediately, he refused to take my advice. He rightly said the decision was his and he would get the earliest plane. This proved difficult, as there was a pile-up of planes at London's Heathrow Airport because of very bad weather conditions. We used all the influence we could muster at this end, and family and friends in London also tried to get Lawrence on a flight. He waited on stand-by at Heathrow for over two days before he was successful.

I really did not think that either of the children would see Percy alive. The night that Gillian arrived at his bedside his pulse was barely perceptible, and he was deeply unconscious. When Gill and I eventually left the hospital and returned to our flat we talked right through the night. How could we help Percy? How could we hasten the end of his sufferings? I think that both of us would have done anything to help him.

Like a miracle, Percy seemed to have returned to us the next morning. Gillian's arrival appeared to have turned the tide, and I felt that all my prayers had been answered. Percy should really have died at this stage, but the excellent medical care he was receiving, his will to live to be with the children again, the prayers of people who cared, or a combination of all these things, kept him alive.

He smiled when he saw Gillian and was happy to know that Lawrence would be arriving the next day. He was later able to record his reactions:

I went through a time of tremendous palliation, with all sorts of drugs which I think knocked the personality right out of me. I felt terrible, and I think that the worst thing to do to any patient is to give him drugs to try and palliate; they may cause him to lose command of the situation. I requested the doctors to remove these drugs from my treatment so that, in spite of being so seriously ill, during the day at least I could talk coherently and maintain my personality. I firmly believe that the worst and the most degrading thing that you can do to a patient is to depersonalize him. These drugs – which were given to me in good faith to help relieve pain, to try to help me feel better with less discomfort, less nausea, less hiccoughing and which may have helped somewhat – upset my dignity. I requested particular drugs for specific symptoms rather than generalized ones for all complaints. When my colleagues adopted this form of treatment, I began to feel like a normal human being again.

Once Percy, in his very hazy state, managed to indicate that he wanted to discontinue the drugs, he became fully conscious and told me that I could take a few hours off-duty. I asked him if he really wanted me to go, and he replied, 'Definitely not, but I know that you'll resign the job if I don't give you some time off.' He was very happy to let Gillian share the day and night 'specialling', which continued for a further four days, as he was still critically ill.

Although I had always been aware of the depth of the feeling that Lawrence and Percy had for each other, they had been unable to communicate, and Lawrence's hasty return to his bedside was a wonderful boost to Percy's morale. Lawrence said later:

> I had long criticized my father for expecting that everyone live by his standards, for demanding too much from others, for failing to recognize human weaknesses, different values. That night when my father lost control of his emotions and I did not want to apologize, I realized how alike we were, how the same criticism I applied to him applied to myself also.
>
> Four months before my Dad passed away I was due to leave on an overseas holiday. Although he was too weak to accompany us to the airport, he spent hours helping me pack, making sure, for the last time, that everything was in order. As I left I was aware that I might have to return home early. As it happened, his condition worsened steadily over the next two months. He was hospitalized again, and I came home, frantically barging my way through airport queues. He was terribly pleased to see me. I knew then how much I had always loved my father.

I spoke to Percy before Lawrence arrived and begged him to lower his usual reserve and let Lawrence know how he really felt about him. The two of them were alone together for an hour, and I have no idea what they discussed, but the end result was something special. Lawrence came out of the room with tears in his eyes and said he would have walked from overseas to have reached this understanding with his father. Percy cried unashamedly. He was so grateful to know that Lawrence really loved him.

Incredibly, Percy's will to live persisted. In spite of the fact that after the operation he required intravenous fluid therapy and occasional nasogastric suction to relieve the symptoms of distension, we began to hope that he might come home once more. On the seventh postoperative day he had a bowel action, which showed that the obstruction was overcome, and from then on his condition began to improve. On the fifteenth postoperative day he was allowed to come home to recuperate.

I never expected this development. The torture of those last days is indescribable, although having all the children with me was a great help. Percy recorded these thoughts:

I persuaded the doctors to let me come home, as I felt so much better. That homecoming was definitely the best day of my life. My experience of this whole illness has now gone over a period of about twenty months. The worst has been the last two months, when I have been very ill. Strange to say, however, even when you are very ill you can still enjoy life, and there are still a lot of things that can be done.

One of the most important things I enjoy is the lovely visitors who come and visit me. Obviously, they have to be organized to come at certain times, but visitors are a magnificent boon. Some visitors are boring and talk only about themselves, but most make life worth while and make everything so enjoyable.

Then, of course, I have a wonderful family. My wife looks after me as no one else possibly could. She has washed me and bathed me, given me magnificent food and made life so comfortable and comforting. These last few days, as I have repeatedly said, have probably been the best days of all my life.

Over this time also my children visited me. One came from Toronto – they sent for her – and my son, who was in Europe, unhesitatingly just came back, and this, of course, was a wonderful bonus . . . In fact, with my whole family around me, stress seems to disappear, and we've had so many hours of laughter and fun that at times we have forgotten about the illness which struck me. Of course, my eldest daughter Michele, who is here, has been absolutely marvellous as well, even though she had to work so hard. [She went back to training school to study midwifery at this stage.] She has given me tremendous support and, as a nurse, has known how to behave towards me. All my children, all three of them, have been so wonderful in giving me their tremendous support. I think that one can learn from serious illness that despite mental trauma, and in spite of dismal prognosis, and in spite of what people say, and in spite of weight loss – in fact, looking almost cachetic [debilitated] at times – you can still enjoy life. You can still have wonderful days, and you can still make use of many hours and spend happy times with your family and friends.

Percy seemed to radiate a feeling of well-being and happiness. I asked him how it was that he had this feeling of well-being. He explained that throughout his whole life he had been so busy doing things, chasing his tail and trying to 'get there' that he had had no time to take a look at all the wonderful things on the way. Now for the first time in his life, and even though he knew his time was limited, he could turn round and look at the wonderful view. He liked what he saw; he felt a complete person, happy with his own contribution to living and very happy for his children and grandchildren. This was the first time in his life that all the fences had been down, and the warmth and love that encircled him made him a very proud man. His happiness spilled over to all of us, and often people remarked that they were amazed at our attitude. They came to call on us expecting to feel sad and depressed, and they left elated. We fitted in more living in those two months than most people do in a whole lifetime. I shall be for ever grateful for this experience.

We had a heightened appreciation of the time that was left, and Percy felt that even though his body was being attacked, his spirit was enriched. In the past I had always had to share Percy with his work and patients. Now we were content just to be together.

Far into the night we discussed everything that had taken place in our lives, including the many mistakes we had made over the years. With the new understanding and sympathy we had for each other we were able to discuss the past without fear, tension or distress. We spoke of our parents, our families and our many wonderful friends. We looked back over all our good fortune and felt grateful for the happy times we had shared. We were able to discuss the hurts we had inflicted upon each other; we talked of their importance at the time and agreed that they were unimportant now. The fact that we were able to talk to each other so freely produced in us both an empathy that perhaps we could never have achieved in any other way. They were golden days for us. Percy was at peace with himself and with all those around him.

During the whole period of Percy's illness the most important therapy for me was taking walks practically every day, even if only for a short while. The sea seemed to heal with its fury and its gentle ripples like the gurgles of a baby. The incessant waxing and waning of the tide carried on regardless, and I always returned at peace and a little humble. Percy wanted to know why these walks were necessary for me, and I explained that there was one spot in particular where I could communicate with God.

Percy had never really believed in God but had always loved Jewish tradition and custom. Towards the end, however, I sensed that his attitude had changed, for he was not so definite in his views. We discussed religion in great detail, particularly the question of life after death. We read many books about this subject. The one that expressed Percy's sentiments best was *Living Jewish* by Michael Asheri, who writes:

About the only thing that can accurately be said about the Jewish concept of life after death is that Jews believe in it. But if you try to pin down just what form their belief takes, you are unlikely to meet with much that is universally applicable. The fact is that when God gave us the Torah, He revealed to Moses how he wanted his commandments obeyed; but in the entire Torah there is not a single word which can literally be taken to refer to life beyond the grave or to a 'world to come'. The emphasis is almost entirely on the observance of God's commandments in the world, and living the way a Jew should but what happens after death we leave in God's hands and He has revealed nothing concerning it. What is basic to Judaism is the belief in an immortal soul given to us by God.

Maurice Lamm, in his book *The Jewish Way in Death and Mourning*, writes that when the coming of the Messiah takes place:

> It will not be a new world, a qualitatively different world, rather will it be this world brought to perfection. Universal peace, tranquillity, lawfulness and goodness will prevail, and all will acknowledge the unity and lordship of God.

He also says:

> with all of modern man's sophistication, his brilliant technological achievements, the immense progress of his science, his discovery of new worlds of thought, he has not come one iota closer to grasping the meaning of death than did his ancient ancestors. Philosophers and poets have probed the idea of immortality, but stubbornly it remains, as always, the greatest paradox of life.

Percy always believed that people who were fortunate enough to have strong religious beliefs were more resigned to the prospect of death. He also believed that what happens in life is of greater importance than delving into death and that as he had gained from the example of others, he hoped that maybe he had also, in some small way, made a contribution to life. He was proud when Lawrence received as a *barmitzvah* present from a very dear friend a pair of binoculars inscribed: 'See the world as your parents see it – with love and compassion.'

Percy had tremendous support from his medical friends, both those attending him and many others. David and Dudley were involved with Percy the person. John was his general practitioner and visited him daily; his presence gave Percy confidence, and he assumed responsibility for decisions. I think they discussed non-medical topics far more than medical ones during the many hours they spent together.

One of our friends made me promise that should a time arrive when Percy needed constant care, she would look after him at night rather than allow him to be sent to hospital. I did not refuse her offer, as I knew how important it was for her to be involved. The doctors called as early as eight in the morning, before they started their general calls. We used to juggle our times to fit in with them when they arrived, but occasionally our plans misfired, and on more than one occasion they sat on top of the toilet-seat cover chatting to Percy while he bathed.

Then there were the regulars, some daily, some weekly. Percy liked me to prepare snacks and drinks so that they could relax and enjoy themselves. There was Bill, who never arrived without his home-grown roses, which started as buds but opened to full bloom with the most beautiful perfume. During the entire period when Percy was no longer working there was never a day when the roses were not in evidence. Barry was a psychiatrist, but he called practically every day as a friend, which both Percy and I appreciated, particularly as he was far from well himself. And Bertie was also very concerned about his friend. The Three Bs, as we called them, were very special people in our lives.

We borrowed a video machine to watch home movies. One evening, after watching a fascinating film for more than three hours, Percy noticed that one of his legs was slightly swollen. During the night it became painful, and the next morning it was extremely swollen. Percy knew that he had developed a femoral thrombosis (a clot of blood in the vein).

I felt that it just was not possible for Percy to suffer any more. I wished that the clot would become dislodged so that his end would come suddenly and finally this time. How wrong these thoughts of mine proved to be. Percy wanted to live, and live he did. When all the odds are stacked against you, it is the easiest thing in the world to fold up and quit, but Percy was so concerned about his leg that I was forced into action. Although in some ways it is a disadvantage to know about all the medical implications, Percy was lucky in knowing what to do just then. En route to the chemist to fetch stretch bandages, I had to run around the building looking for bricks to lift the end of the bed.

John the general practitioner phoned David the surgeon, and arrangements were made to admit Percy to hospital once again. This time it was almost a pleasure, as Percy's condition was something entirely different. Percy was put on a machine for regulating a drug that was used to thin the blood. It made a bleeping sound when it was not functioning properly. Michele knew just what to do, and she was very peeved when Percy refused to acknowledge that she was competent to cope with the situation and insisted on calling the assistant nurse!

There was no tension on this occasion. Percy was full of nonsense, and we teased him unmercifully. He nagged David to let him go home, and when David finally gave his permission Percy virtually jumped out of bed with a whoop of delight.

We had another two and a half wonderful weeks before us. Percy described them thus:

> I do so enjoy the lovely flat in which we live and the beautiful view of the sea, with the sun streaming in from all angles . . .
>
> Another difficult thing to do . . . is to try and get your affairs in order. This is more difficult than you probably think. I had to do this in a hurry, and I think I learned a tremendous lesson. We, as men, often just carry out affairs without telling anyone else how we do things. I think it is very important that, whatever we do, we should tell our wives and explain exactly what we have done, what we anticipate, how to plan things and what we hope to achieve. I was lucky now, with these days available to me, to be able to discuss all my affairs with my wife and family, so that I now have no problems, no worries about my affairs and how things work out.

Although in the past Percy had always wanted to discuss his business affairs with me I had never been really interested. Now I realized how important this was for his peace of mind, so I wrote down all his instructions. He was meticulous and wanted me to understand the whole position. He arranged for his insurance agent to call and asked him to explain to me the details of the various policies. Apparently this was the first time that the agent had ever been requested to do such a thing, and he was astounded. Percy's accountant – a cousin but, more important, a friend – was extremely kind and was available at all times. He even came to the hospital to discuss something that was bothering Percy. Through both these men I learned all the details of Percy's business affairs.

After this was all settled, Percy was at ease and asked me if I was pleased with the way in which the details had been worked out. But how could I possibly feel anything other than despair about these arrangements for my future after Percy's death? Percy, on the other hand, was very philosophical and said that he was pleased that the end had not come suddenly, as it had in the case of Morris and, particularly, Norman. However heartsore I was while discussing the inevitable, he convinced me that I should take pleasure in his peace of mind.

Percy spent hours each day writing letters to his friends and colleagues overseas, telling them of his terminal illness and bidding them farewell. He even received replies to some of these letters, which made him very happy. One was from the trial co-ordinator of the Ludwig Institute for Cancer Research:

> It is impossible for me to express my feeling about your remark that the disease from which you suffer is not under control. There is very little I can say. I am extremely sorry that I did not have the opportunity to work along with you from the beginning of the Ludwig Breast Cancer Studies. I will certainly make sure that everything you mention in your letter is arranged and, of course, will keep you informed about the trial – which now in February has begun to proceed according to our plans. It is clear that your initiative, your work and constant application, your rare spirit, have set the standard for the activities of the entire Group, and for this, dear Percy, I would like to thank you from the bottom of my heart.

Although Percy cried when he received this reply, he said that he had a wonderful sense of achievement, which previously he would not have acknowledged.

Percy's leg troubled him somewhat, but we still went for short walks and spent time on the bench opposite our flat overlooking the sea. We shared the discovery that priorities change according to circumstances. Without any anger or sadness Percy remarked that before he would have been interested only in when and where the next international meeting would take place; now he was content to sit in the sun and watch the waves breaking continuously against the rocks.

In the evenings we laughed at old slides and argued about whether they showed Hyde Park or Kew Gardens. We still played the odd rubber of bridge, and our friends never stopped coming.

To the end Percy's surgeon, David, remained one of his favourite visitors. David was also a very private person, and he and Percy got on very well, as in many ways their views and reactions were similar. Whether Percy did not want to share David with others or whether he thought that David would prefer to relax with us on our own I am still uncertain. Whichever was the case, if we knew David was calling, we arranged things so that we entertained him alone, and each time he came, Percy behaved like a small·child enjoying a special treat.

Percy's condition began to deteriorate. However little I gave him to eat, he was unable to enjoy it. His abdomen was becoming very distended, and his bowels were not functioning. I gave him a small enema, but there was no result. By mutual consent we said nothing about the significance of these symptoms, but we both knew that the dreaded time was approaching. One morning when Percy awoke he said, 'I think you had better contact David.'

I travelled with Percy in the ambulance. We knew that this was to be our last journey together. We held hands, and tears rolled down our cheeks. When we reached the hospital Percy thanked the driver for the care with which he had driven us.

There was no delay as Percy was readmitted to Ward B1 that Sunday morning. His symptoms were relieved when the excess fluid was removed from his abdomen and an intravenous infusion was connected to replace the loss of fluids and to which could be added medication for pain. Soon he was sleeping peacefully.

I watched him, my mind in a turmoil. I was worried about his awaking, but my fears were unnecessary. I am convinced that nature creates around the very old and the seriously ill a buffer that protects them from fear and anxiety. Percy was absolutely resigned to his condition and was happy to have around him people who were looking after his welfare.

After a few days he felt much better and requested the doctors to remove the nasogastric tube and disconnect the intravenous infusion, which they did, but his physical reaction was disastrous. His abdomen became distended again; he felt nauseous and started vomiting. He knew that his vague hopes of coming home one more time were over.

He consoled me by telling me not to worry on his behalf. He knew the score exactly, and he was quite happy and content with me at his bedside. As long as he knew that he would not have to suffer unnecessary discomforts or indignities, he wanted nothing more.

He was not allowed visitors at this time, as he was heavily sedated and slept for long periods. While he was asleep he looked like a dying man, but as soon as he was awake he became alert, interested as well as interesting, and he wanted to know everything that was going on. The children and his sister Nancy came regularly, and Michele popped in whenever she could, often late at night, just to reassure herself and me that he was comfortable. I spent all day with him and often stayed long into the night, as he was loth to let me go.

At one stage it was thought inadvisable to allow small children to visit seriously ill patients, but Michele felt that the grandchildren were so concerned about Percy that it would be better for them to see him for themselves than to conjure up weird thoughts in their minds. Adie and Larry were very nervous at the thought of visiting Percy, but once they realized that he was still the same Grandpa, they examined everything with great interest, while Percy explained to them the purpose of various medical aids.

After a short while the two children were completely at ease, and they began telling Percy all about what they had been doing. It was a pleasure to watch Percy enjoying his grandchildren's company.

One might imagine that Percy would no longer have been interested in the intravenous fluids and what they contained, but he checked every bottle/bag, the speed at which it was running and whether his fluid balance was correct. He made quite sure that he was getting enough electrolytes (essential components of body fluid) to keep him going, and he kept the nursing staff on their toes. The probationer nurses were sitting their examinations just then, so while they were washing him in the mornings he gave them tutorials, which they said helped them tremendously.

The quality of nursing, from the most junior to the most senior, was superb, and the empathy that flowed between patient and staff was almost tangible. The doctors could not have given him more care if he had been a member of their own families, a fact of which Percy was fully aware. David, in particular, gave Percy a zest for life. I noticed that even when Percy was in a deep sleep, the second that David came into the room he became wide awake and alert.

One night I felt that I could not leave Percy, even though he was in excellent hands. Imagine my surprise when, at nearly midnight, David appeared at the door. He had been to a party and had come to see how Percy was. He spent nearly an hour with me in the little side-ward discussing how we could make him more comfortable. Rather apologetically, I made some suggestions. He agreed with them at once: he said that he saw the patient for only a short time daily, while I was there all the time and was more aware of his needs. David was prepared to try anything to improve matters. One of the points I made was that although Percy insisted on getting out of bed to pass urine, the effort was now too much for him. At David's suggestion he consented to have a catheter inserted. This was something that Percy had dreaded from the time of his original operation, but once he was able to adjust to circumstances, the catheter made a great difference to his comfort.

Indeed, Percy felt so much more comfortable that he even showed an interest in a forthcoming cricket match that was being televised. I was so excited that I arranged to have a full-size colour television set delivered to his room. The hospital area is known to have very poor reception, so I also ordered an enormous aerial to improve the quality of the picture. As we all waited for the big moment the comings and goings of the technicians, the doctors and the nurses reminded me of the Marx Brothers in *A Night at the Opera*. Imagine our disappointment when the machine was turned on and there was no picture. Fortunately, a patient in an adjoining ward insisted that Percy borrow her small black-and-white portable set, which worked perfectly!

Everyone was extremely kind. I laughed one day when I came upon two of the most senior matrons at the hospital shaking up Percy's cushions and making him comfortable, and John, the professor of surgery, never left the hospital without seeing Percy. It was acts of warmth and generosity like these that gave such a wonderful quality to the last days of his life.

His condition now began to deteriorate rapidly. Normal intravenous therapy had to be discontinued, as his veins had collapsed. A central venous line that went through the neck directly to the heart was inserted by a specialist. Percy was thrilled, as this left his arms and legs completely free, and he was much more comfortable. He even laughingly told me to be careful while I was washing him, as he had only one life left on the other side of his neck. Instead of being in a state about the procedure, he marvelled at the advances in medicine.

Although Percy was very philosophical about his condition, I was rapidly reaching a stage of despair, and one morning I confessed to Lawrence that I wished the end would come. Lawrence said kindly but firmly, 'Ma, don't talk nonsense. You know in your heart of hearts you could not wish Dad dead. Go and put on your face and go to the hospital, where he is waiting for you.' When I entered Percy's room and saw his expression I realized that Lawrence was right – I wanted Percy to go on living as long as possible.

It was at this stage that a nursing sister with whom Percy had been very friendly called on him. During the conversation she said, 'Well, Percy, the cards are on the table. Tell me, what would you do with your life if you had your time all over again?' He contemplated the question for some time and answered, 'I would spend much more time talking to my patients.'

I wonder if Percy decided he had had enough on the day that a pressure sore (bedsore) started, and it became too painful for him to move. He said goodbye to Michele three times when she called at lunchtime. He chatted to David for a long time when he came to see him in the afternoon. In the early hours of the next morning he squeezed my hand and smiled his beautiful smile. Then he closed his eyes and went to sleep for ever.

It was a grey day. Everything was grey – the sea, the sky, the mountains in the distance. The sea was like a sheet of glass; there were no ripples as the water met the rocks. There was no traffic on the road, although cars normally roared past at this time in the morning. Everywhere there was an unearthly hush.

I cried as I said goodbye to my darling. This time my tears were for myself and not for my dearest husband, who had come to peace and was beyond all suffering. (I remember a phrase I once read: 'Grief is the price we pay for loving.') The anguish in my heart was the knowledge that I would never see or touch him again. Then I reached a haven in my mind. I remember thinking that blossoms fall when they are at the height of their beauty, and I felt comforted as I thought of the closeness we had all achieved during the past two years.

Percy and I had been able to speak freely of all our thoughts. Lawrence and Percy had been able to express the love they had for each other. Although he had died prematurely, Percy had been able to reap the rewards of all his endeavours. I felt a deep sense of gratitude for his life and for the time we had spent together.

It was this sense of gratitude that prompted me to write our story. If one person derives from our experiences comfort and the strength to strive for the same dignity in living and dying that Percy enjoyed, I know he would have been satisfied.

Grief and Comfort: the Struggle for Acceptance

Percy had discussed with me the arrangements for his funeral, and I carried out all his requests. There followed the week of *Shiva*, a period of mourning observed by Jews after a funeral. During the week prayers are said for the soul of the departed, and people call on the bereaved family constantly, so that they are never alone. It is not the custom to bring flowers; visitors usually arrive with cakes and other kinds of food, thus relieving the family of the duties of hospitality. It is a time for talking about the person who has died. Shared memories bring tears and renew sadness, but they often prompt smiles and even gentle laughter too.

Although we were emotionally prepared for Percy's death, and perhaps had even wished for it at times, the pain of its finality was very acute. At first I felt that the pain belonged to me alone, but many of Percy's patients and friends needed to share their grief with me, and I realized that his death had severed a link in their lives as well. I made a few exceptional friends at that time – people whom I would probably never have met in normal circumstances. They, together with our old friends and my wonderful family, helped to heal the gaping wound in my heart. Then there were the letters of condolence that arrived from far and wide, some of them from people whom I did not even know. The beautiful sentiments they expressed often brought fresh tears. Obituaries were published in professional journals all over the world. The following extract is taken from one written by Ronald Raven, Percy's old 'chief' at the Royal Marsden Hospital in London, which appeared in *Clinical Oncology*:

This short account of the life and work of Percy Helman will include a warm tribute to the man himself, whom I knew and whose friendship I valued for thirty years. His company was always a most pleasurable experience, for he was happy, genial, full of professional enthusiasm, interested in everything and loved life at its best. Percy was a gentle man, kind and considerate for others, and a splendid doctor. He had an abiding and deep compassion for patients and all who suffered and taught the importance of respecting the human dignity of everyone. That which he preached he also practised. He enjoyed the happiest family life with his charming wife Ethel – a trained nurse – two daughters, a son and two grandchildren. His elder daughter is a trained nurse and the younger daughter a doctor. During his long illness he was surrounded and supported by tender loving care and during this anxious period he even returned to work for a time. Throughout his courage never faltered and there was no complaint. I recall his letter to me stating that he had put all his affairs in perfect order and was ready for the call. I know how many there are who will join me in saying, 'Well done, Percy, good and faithful. May you enjoy eternal rest in that other world of peace.'

The love, concern and support of people who had known Percy, professionally or personally, were invaluable to me. Inevitably, however, I had to try to come to terms with my own private sorrow. It is important to be able to express grief, so that it does not fester like a sore inside one. It is equally important to allow the healing process to take its own time. It can be very distressing to be told, however kindly, to 'pull yourself together', when all you long for is to *feel* 'together' again. The platitude 'Time is a wonderful healer' is to some extent true, but often, for no particular reason, unbearable grief engulfs the bereaved. People cope with their sorrow in different ways; I believe that we should all be willing to accept, from no matter what source, any help that will enable us to face the future positively.

I write this feelingly, as soon after Percy died I had an

experience that I would have ridiculed once, when I was sceptical about anything that did not have an obvious explanation.

It was a black and stormy day. The rain was pouring down on to an angry, wild sea, and the wind was hissing through tiny cracks in the window frames. I was sitting at Percy's desk, typing his story.

Suddenly the clouds parted and the sun poured into the room, blinding me. I had the most peculiar feeling that Percy was standing behind my chair and caressing my neck with his hands. I visualized him smiling down at me in approval of what I was typing. At that moment the telephone on the desk rang and the voice of an unknown woman said, 'I just want you to know that your husband has not left us. He is with us now.'

I felt as if an electric current had passed through me and I had become detached from my body. I told the caller that it was strange that she had telephoned just then, as I was writing about Percy. 'Yes, I know,' she said. 'I am a patient of his, and he has given me the courage to carry on living.' As I replaced the receiver, the sky clouded over again and the rain continued to fall as if it had never ceased.

It took me a few minutes to compose myself. I wondered whether I had imagined the whole incident. Was it what I wanted to believe? Was it pure coincidence, or did it have any deeper meaning? I do not know the answer, and I do not particularly care. The fact remains that it made me very happy at the time.

Whatever the explanation of that curious incident, one thing is certain: I am not alone in my conviction that Percy's gentle influence and zest for life will long outlive his death. It is to David that I willingly give the final word:

> It is extraordinarily difficult to write about Percy. I have a type of schizophrenia which has him both dead and living. Yes, he suffered a severe illness and died from it, yet the image that I evoke when I think of him has him well, very well indeed, asking, relating, laughing, providing homily, listening, encouraging and, in a quiet, bubbling way, enjoying the business of living.

Epilogue

Since Percy's death I have become associated with St Luke's Hospice, Cape Town, the first hospice to be established in South Africa, founded on lines similar to those of hospices in the United Kingdom. As with other hospices, it is open to all regardless of colour, class, creed or social standing. The hospice started as a home-care service in June 1983. In October 1985 in-patient facilities and a day-care centre were opened in a beautiful old home in Kenilworth in the Cape. All volunteers and workers attend lectures, seminars and workshops, where the fundamental principles of hospice care – namely, caring, sharing, listening and being there – are explored and discussed with a view to determining how they may best be translated into practical care.

I became involved with the hospice because I hoped to be able to give. In fact, I have probably received more from it than from any formal training. It is a truism that in offering love, care and compassion to patients with fatal illnesses, one receives much in return without realizing it. I was able to give my all to Percy; now I am glad to be able to share in the task of caring for other patients, in the hope that my experience may help to relieve their suffering.